LUNCHTIME CHRONICLES
Issue 59

He likes
his woman
thick, tender,
and ready to
melt in
his *mouth*...

RUMP ROAST

LaQuette

ISBN: 978-1-948937-17-7

Edition Number: 1ST edition 2023

Rump Roast

by

LaQuette

Dedication

To anyone who's ever left a great love behind, it's never too late to spin the block.

Blurb

H e likes his woman thick, tender, and ready to melt in his mouth...

The last thing Najah Temple needs is the walking distraction that is Tomasso Moretti. Not when her event planning business needs her full attention.

When Tomasso offers her an incredible business opportunity that she can't possibly turn down, Najah finds herself in a compromising position. But how is a woman supposed to keep her eyes on her bag when Tomaso is dripping sex appeal like it's his job? And once she remembers what he tastes like, how can she be expected to stay away?

Najah Temple's sexy-as-sin lips may say she doesn't want Tomaso Moretti, but the sultry fire in her gaze when she looks at him says something altogether different. He lost her fifteen years ago and he's not above using a fake engagement and a business opportunity to find his way back into her heart.

She's matured into delicious bronzed temptation on legs. And ass man that he is, Tomasso certainly can't ignore her perfectly shaped rump in those painted-on jeans. As far as he's concerned, there is no way in hell he's gonna walk away from a chance to finally have her back where she belongs: in his arms and his bed.

Chapter 1

"**F**ucking perfect."

Tomasso Moretti sat quietly in the corner as he watched the object of his desire milling about the grand ballroom as she directed staff and appraised their execution of her orders.

Gone was the quiet, studious girl who'd stolen his heart the moment he'd seen her freshman year of high school. In her place was a boss, running her business, getting the damn job done. Watching her run shit with a clipboard in one hand, a pen in the other, while on a pair of do-me heels, was divine.

After fifteen years, Najah Temple wore her confidence like a badge. That in and of itself was enough to keep his eyes glued to her. But the sight of her full curves in that red romper meant he couldn't pull his gaze away from her if he'd wanted.

Tomasso came from a big Italian family that loved everything in abundance. Food, family, and fun were all big, brilliant, and fabulous things to be thoroughly enjoyed to the fullest. It was how he lived his life, and how he loved his woman. And as the fitted material of the romper caressed Najah's voluptuous curves and put all that ass on display, there wasn't a chance in hell Tomasso was going to give up the glorious view he had.

He'd waited fifteen years for this moment, to reclaim what was always his. Fifteen years of fulfilling a promise that had kept him away from her, and now that this moment had arrived, he was going to enjoy every damn second of it. Too bad poor Najah hadn't a clue what she was in for.

***

Najah Temple took in a breath as she surveyed the work she and her team had done.

"Perfection."

That was the only word to describe the way her team had turned the ship's grand ballroom into a tropical oasis with billowy tulle-covered pillars, soft uplighting of blues, greens, and purplish lights that made the room look like it was submerged beneath the Caribbean Sea.

The tables were covered with light blue linens, and the large center-pieces of tropical florals were the perfect accents to the themed decor.

Najah stood back, taking it all in, loving what her vision and her team's execution had created. She had a right to be proud. Not just of the decor of this room, or any of the events she'd organized for this alumni cruise, but of the business she'd built one brick at a time.

Her business was thriving after a rough start, and now she was slowly moving her way up to larger and more prestigious accounts. The Excelsior High School Alumni Association was her largest client to date. After the terrific way things had unfolded over the last week, she was sure she'd be adding another repeat customer to her client list.

"You always did enjoy admiring your own work."

Najah's entire body stilled at the sound of that familiar voice. It was deeper, richer than it had been when they were teenagers, at the exclusive Excelsior together. Then, it made her heart dance and her insides bubble with giddiness. Now, it made heat tickle her skin as it washed over her.

Has it been so long since you've had any that the sound of an old flame's voice makes your lady parts tingle?

"It's good to see you again, Najah."

She slowly turned around to find all six feet four inches of Tomasso Moretti's solid and brawny frame standing in front of her.

In a tailored Armani suit that hung perfectly on his large shoulders, he sucked up all the air in the room, making it hard for her to focus on anything else but him.

"Tomasso," she whispered, afraid that if she spoke louder, her nerves would betray her, and her voice would crack. "I wasn't aware you'd be here. Your name wasn't on the manifest."

"Considering my family's company owns the vessel, I felt it was finally time for me to show my face at one of these things."

He smiled, and his crisp blue eyes lit up, softening the hard plains of his face. He touched his hand to his neatly trimmed beard that gave his classically handsome features a bit of a rugged edge.

As sexy as he was with his beard and big body, it wasn't either of those things that had her fighting to stay upright. It was those bright eyes of his, specifically, how they moved over the length of her with visible appreciation.

"Time has been good to you," he said as he lifted his gaze and met hers. "But then again, you were always the prettiest girl in the room at Excelsior."

His comment broke whatever spell he'd cast over her that made her stand still, waiting for his next word.

"Me? The prettiest girl at Excelsior? I think you might have some kind of fever clouding your memories. Everyone except you avoided me like being poor was contagious."

He stepped closer, snaking his fingers around hers as he picked up her hand.

"Najah, always so book smart, yet oblivious to the world around you. The boys kept their distance because once we started dating, I threatened to snap anyone's neck who even glanced at you."

He lifted her hand to his lips and pressed a whisper of kiss there that had her ready to swoon.

To hell with it, she definitely was swooning. The mix of his soft but masculine cologne, the heat of his skin touching hers, coupled with his heated blue gaze was enough to make any woman who liked dick a little dizzy.

It had always been this way between them. Even when they were teenagers who knew nothing about love, the moment they'd locked gazes, they'd been joined at the hip for four straight years.

He touched his hand to the small of her back, bringing her back to the present. She stiffened, not because his touch bothered her, but because she wanted more of it. And right now, with this gig being so close to finishing, being distracted by errant desires of Tomasso touching her just would not do.

"I...I," she stammered, trying to make her tongue speak intelligible words. "I think you're mistaken."

He shook his head, still pinning her with his eyes. "Nope. I'm not. In fact, I have proof."

"Proof?" Her skeptical brow raised trying to figure out what kind of proof he could possibly have.

"In fifteen years, I've never attended one of these alumni events, let alone volunteered one of my businesses as a venue."

"I don't understand how that's proof, Tomasso."

He stepped even closer, their bodies almost touching as he leaned down to whisper in her ear.

"I'm here because I knew you were going to be here. We've got some unfinished business, you and I."

She could feel the vee forming between her brows as confusion muddled her brain.

"Do we? As far as I remember, our business ended when you broke up with me because, and I quote, "You don't fit into my world, Najah. It's time for me to move on with someone else who does.""

That painful memory that she'd worked so hard to forget resurfaced with precise clarity. She looked up into his eyes, expecting to see the cold gaze she remembered from that day. But all she saw was remorse and what looked like...shame?

Whatever it was, it flickered brightly for a second and then it was gone, and in its place was conviction and fire.

"That was not my finest moment. I owe you the biggest of apologies for how I ended things. I was a stupid kid with a lot going on in his head. Instead of saying that, I took the easy way out and blamed it on our differences instead."

He placed a finger under her chin, making sure she was looking directly at him.

"I'm sorry, Najah."

"You came all the way here to apologize to me?" He smiled down at her like he had a secret that she wasn't privy to.

"Najah, I had every intention of apologizing to you when I found you. But that's not the reason I came here."

"Then what is?"

He paused, cupping her cheek, and stroking the skin there.

"I came for you, Najah." He stood there with determination etched into his features as he continued, "And I intend to have you."

Chapter 2

B *reathe, Najah. Just breathe.*

Najah repeated the litany that her late grandma Jeanie used to whisper to her every time she was afraid or worried about something.

She needed that control right now. She wasn't afraid. But she was damn sure worried about losing control to the man in front of her.

Tomasso Moretti, sex on legs, just told her he intended to have her. And by the way he'd let the tip of his tongue swipe over his bottom lip, she was pretty sure it didn't have anything to do with a single item on the alumni event itinerary.

Nope, she didn't need this right now. She absolutely did not need this. She was here to do a thing to build her business. Having this sexy, rich man "have her" whatever the hell that meant, was not on the agenda, no matter how much she wanted it to be.

And just to be clear, she definitely did want it to be.

His silky deep voice had already awakened desire in her. The idea of him acting on his stated intention had her folds slick and her pussy aching for attention.

Nope, she had to be an adult, and her kitty would just have to behave her thirsty ass, because Tomasso was off limits.

He'd broken her heart once, and she'd be damned if she gave him the opportunity to do it again. Back then, she was young, and her heart eventually stitched itself back together after he'd smashed it with a sledgehammer.

Fortified with logic and determination, she started to pull away, but then he played dirty and did the one thing she hadn't expected him to, at least not in a room full of their former classmates.

He leaned down, placing a gentle kiss at the corner of her mouth, just shy of where she wanted it to be.

She opened her mouth to speak but was distracted by the feel of Tomasso's strong arm tugging Najah against his body.

And then, his lips were against hers.

His lips were soft and gentle against flesh. To anyone looking, it probably looked like a friendly peck, but when he let that deep moan of satisfaction slip into the air, heat rose within her and she lifted her hands to his face, loving the soft feel of his beard against her skin.

Tomasso Moretti was kissing her, and she was kissing him back, and they were both enjoying it.

When he finally set her free, Najah took a steadying breath before trying to step back, yet again. Well, she told her feet to move, but they'd decided now was the time they wouldn't listen.

"Going somewhere, Sweetness?"

God that voice saying that name. It was smooth and rich like an aged whiskey that you wanted to sip and savor. And lord knew she wanted to sip and savor that man. He'd given her that name and she'd answered to it every time because it was a gift from him to her.

"Tomasso, I appreciate the apology. But you don't have to pour it on that thick. We were over a long time ago. I don't need this performance. It's water under the bridge."

"Performance?" He placed his finger under her chin, locking gazes with her. "There's no act, Sweetness. I told you; I came here for you."

"Tomasso," she let her hands drop down to his forearms as she stepped out of his embrace. "I need to get back to work."

He stepped into her personal space again, and it took everything she had not to retreat.

"You can't run from me, Sweetness. We're on a boat surrounded by water."

He did have a point. They'd be at sea for the next two days until they returned to port.

She made the mistake of running her tongue over her bottom lip and now she could swear she could still feel the ghost of his kiss.

"Have dinner with me tonight, Sweetness, and I promise, I'll explain all of it to you then."

"And if I don't?"

The corner of his mouth hitched up as he ran a careful hand over his beard.

"Well, if you don't come to me, I'll be forced to come to you. And I doubt you'll get much work done with me underfoot."

A quick glance around the room and she could see the attendees mulling around the room. She had to be on her A-game tonight with so much at stake with this account.

And Tomasso, with his big muscles and irreverent smile was one hell of a distraction she couldn't afford.

"Fine," she replied. "I'll have dinner with you."

Chapter 3

"Is everything to your liking sir?"

Tomasso looked at the elegantly set table near the large, windowed wall of his luxury suite. The suite was positioned at the bridge of the ship, giving the illusion that you were right on top of the water.

Tomasso glanced at the large silver serving platters and the champagne chilling in the ice bucket before he nodded, giving his blessing to the service butler.

The stately man dressed in an all-white suit lit the candles in the center of the table and left as quietly as he'd come.

Making quick work of the champagne cork, he poured himself a glass and moved over to the window's edge. The moonlight glinted off the deep blue waves, and out here, with the gentle sway of the ship, life almost seemed serene.

There was nothing ahead of him, nothing to see beyond the darkness staring back at him. It was soothing. Something he wished he could hold onto beyond this moment, something he wished he could carry into his reality when he stepped off this boat.

As the oldest son of Ernesto Moretti, he was born to be his father's successor at The Triple M Corporation. He'd resigned himself to that fact a long time ago. He'd just believed he had more time to live the life he'd wanted, even if it was temporary.

His cellphone came alive in his pocket and Tomasso tensed. He didn't pull it out to see who was calling. He didn't need to. The same person had been calling him for days now.

The upside of being rich was that you could afford cellular service that could work in the most remote places in the world. The bad thing was that meant his father could reach him and pull him back to his side with just a phone call.

A knock at the door pulled him out of his musings, making him focus on the here and now. For now, he was away from his father, away from all the responsibilities that would befall him, away from the life that had already been planned from his first breath.

Now, Najah was here. His present was here, and if only for this moment, that had to be good enough.

Tomasso took another sip of his drink, setting the glass down on the table, and then opened the door.

His chest tightened at the sight of her. She'd changed out of the red romper she'd had on earlier and was now wearing a black maxi dress that left her dark brown shoulders bare, and every curve she possessed on display.

"You've dragged me up here," she muttered, leaning against the door, making her hip jut out. "I hope you have a reason for it."

A reason? He could name a thousand. All of them ending with his hands all over every inch of her glorious skin.

He looked down and the tempting round flesh of her hip called to him. His palm itched to touch it, grip it, use it to pull her against him. He took a calming breath. Later, if everything worked out the way he planned, he'd have all the time in the world to live out his fantasies where this gorgeous woman was concerned. But first, he had to get past the caution he could see filling her eyes.

"Come inside and see, Sweetness."

He stepped aside, standing at the door as he watched her walk inside.

Najah was a beautiful woman. Long, bountiful dark curls framed her face, dark brown skin that looked as smooth as silk, and a set of full lips that he knew could make a man weep if he were so lucky to have them grace his skin.

And then there was her body.

She had full breasts and endless curves. She had a body made for loving, and he'd wanted to, once again, be the lucky man doing that loving. That was especially true of her ass. He was a pig, he knew it. But Najah had an ass that wouldn't quit, and if she ever gave him the opportunity again, he sure as hell wouldn't quit once he got his hands on it.

"Stop watching my ass, Tomasso and tell me why you insisted I have dinner with you."

Her candor made him laugh. She had him dead to rights. There was no use pretending she didn't.

"Woman, you came here in that dress looking that good, there's no way you expected me not to look at your ass."

She turned around with a sly smile that told him his assumption was absolutely correct.

He took a few long strides, and he was beside her, placing his hand on the small of her back to lead her toward the table. He held out a chair for her. Once she was seated comfortably, he poured her a glass of champagne and took the seat beside her.

"This is a really nice spread, Tomasso. You didn't have to go through all this trouble for me. My palate isn't as refined as yours."

"Everything about you is refined. Always has been, Najah."

Her eyes narrowed and he could see the distrust in them. He'd put that distrust there. Now it was time for him to remove it.

"Listen, Tomasso," she held up her hand as he sat down looking as if she was ready to sprint. "If this," she swirled her finger in the direction of the table. "is some stunt to prank the scholarship kid for old time's sake, how 'bout we don't and just say we did?"

***

Fire. Pure fire. That's what she saw when she looked into his eyes. He was...angry. She could see it in the way his body tensed, the way muscle in his jaw ticked.

She was in a room with a man she hadn't seen in fifteen years and his body was tensing up like she'd struck him. And yet, fear didn't well up in her.

He was angry, but controlled, and it gave her a sense of calm she certainly shouldn't have around Tomasso.

"Don't ever say anything like that in my presence again, Najah." His words were clipped, and his lips were flattened into a line. "I never treated you like you were less than me because I came from money, and you didn't. And I never once allowed any of the assholes in our class to disrespect you in front of me either. You were my girl, and if they had a problem with you, they had a problem with me."

She let out a breath, relaxing into her seat before lifting her eyes to his again.

"You're right. You always treated me well. I shouldn't have spoken to you like that. It's just, this cruise has gone well up until now. I don't want anything to mess it up. Landing Excelsior as a recurring client would be huge for my business."

She could see the anger bleeding out of him as he leaned forward.

"Sweetness, I just want to reconnect after all these years."

He smiled at her. It was sexy and brilliant, warming her to her core, and as inviting as a fire on a cold snowy night.

"Tomasso?"

She folded her arms and tilted her head. She might be slightly buzzed by his sex appeal, but she wasn't stupid. No one went this hard over their high school sweetheart.

"You were always too smart for your own good, Najah."

"What's going on, Tomasso? You didn't come all the way on this boat just to rekindle anything with me. Be straight with me. What's happening?"

"I'm in need of a fiancée."

Her mouth dropped open.

"And there's no one else I'd trust to take on that role other than you."

She burst into laughter. She leaned back in her chair, placing a hand on her stomach as she continued to chuckle.

"As much as I'd love to continue this...whatever this is, I can't afford the distraction."

"Distraction?"

He placed his hand on the outside of her thigh. It wasn't overtly sexual, but it was intimate, and it was definitely making her skin tingle.

"That means you're interested in me too?"

Najah shook her head at his silliness. "I think the fact that I kissed you in front of a room full of people was evidence of that."

"Mmm," he hedged. I don't know, I think I might need a little more convincing on the matter."

She leaned forward, meeting him over the corner of the table, and as soon as she was within reach, his lips were on hers.

The hand on her thigh moved up swirling circles over her bare skin, adding to the electricity that seemed to ignite the longer he touched her. He ended the kiss, placing his forehead against hers.

"Are you convinced now?"

"I'm certainly on the way." His answer made her smile, and the mirthful gleam in his eye put her at ease. "Come on, Sweetness. I really do need your help. All you have to do is pretend to be my loving fiancée for six months so that my father will name me as his successor in the company. If you help me out of this jam, I've found myself in, I'll sign you on as the event planner of record for Triple M for the next year. You'll make a shit ton of money. Being able to put that on your resume, with a positive reference from me, and it's like the checks will write themselves for you."

He stretched out a hand, and she let it linger in the air. She didn't know the details and she was sure it wasn't as simple as Tomasso was making it out to be. But making that kind of money and having a reference from Tomasso, that was career, hell, life changing.

She closed her hand around his and tried her best to ignore the voice in her head that warned her nothing in her life had ever been this easy, and this probably would prove to be the rule instead of the exception.

Fuck it. A win is a win.

Chapter 4

"So, tell me why exactly you need a fake fiancée in the first place."

Tomasso looked over at Najah sitting next to him in his Range Rover.

This wasn't the first time she'd ridden shotgun in a car with him. The first person he'd driven when he'd passed his driver's test three months before graduation was Najah.

Unlike states that allowed kids to get their license at sixteen, you had to wait until eighteen in New York. Sure, you could get a junior license before that. But you were restricted to driving to and from school. His father knew he would never abide by that, so he wouldn't let Tomasso take his driver's test until he was eighteen.

Back then, he could reach across the console and rub his hand across her thigh. But the way her shoulder was damn near embedded into the door, he didn't think he should try that just now.

"You know my dad and his two business partners started Triple M before I was born. They took it from a single meat market in Brooklyn and turned it into one of the largest food distribution companies in the country."

She nodded as she spoke, silently encouraging him to continue.

"My dad, he recently found out he's got some health concerns to deal with." Her eyes widened as she sat up straighter in her seat. "He's fine, Najah. But stress could put him at risk for some nasty complications. His doctor advised him to retire. Unfortunately, the way their partnership agreement is set up, he has to let his partners buy him out, or get their approval to sell his share of the partnership to someone else. Dad has put his heart and soul into that place. It's his legacy and he wants to keep it in the family."

She shrugged, but he kept her eyes on him as he spoke.

"So why doesn't your dad just name you as his successor? I'm sure his partners would approve."

If only it were that simple.

"My dad and his partners, they're old school. I do good work for the company. But I'm thirty-three and single, and I haven't brought any prospects around. To them, that means I'm not reliable. Not family business material."

"Is your brother still an entitled, skirt-chasing prick?"

He chuckled as he rounded the corner, turning into his parents' Brookeville driveway. Even though the company was ridiculously successful by the time Tomasso had finished middle school, his parents had refused to leave their Mills Basin home in Brooklyn until both Tomasso and his brother Freddy had graduated high school.

Now, they were living in a large colonial in Long Island, with a pool in the back, enjoying the fruits of all their hard work.

"Freddy is still an asshole, and as much as they feel my lack of a wife makes me unreliable, they know damn well Freddy ruins everything he touches."

"So, you're your father's only hope?"

He parked the car, taking a deep breath before he turned to her.

"I am. I can't let all he's worked for disappear without at least trying to save it. I can't let them force him out."

She ran her hands up and down her thighs before she turned in her seat and placed her hand over his. "Your parents were always nice to me when we were dating. Even though your dad was this big shot, he never made me feel out of place because I was a scholarship kid. That meant something to me."

She didn't say anything more. She didn't have to. From the squeeze of her fingers and the softness in her dark brown eyes, he knew she was invested.

"All right, Moretti. Let's go get this fake engagement underway, then."

That was his girl. The one who was always down for whatever when it came to people she cared about. She was about to reach for the door, but he held on to her hand, keeping her seated.

He rooted around in his jacket pocket until his fingers grasped the cool metal.

"I hope this meets your approval."

Before she could respond, he slid the four-carat pear-shaped diamond on her finger before he pressed a gentle kiss to her hand.

Her eyes were wide and fixed on the large stone. She shook her head slightly and he held up a hand to stop whatever she was about to say.

"Nothing is too much or too good for you, Sweetness. Even if it is for a fake engagement."

***

"Oh, my goodness, Najah!"

Arleen Moretti grabbed Najah in a bear hug and squeezed for all she was worth. Najah melted into the woman's arms just like she had when Najah was a teenager.

Almost every day for four years, Najah had gone home with Tomasso after school, and his mother would greet her like this, like she was family and belonged there.

"Mrs. Moretti," Najah squealed. "It's so good to see you."

Arleen held Najah back, pouting her lips as she stared at her. "What is this Mrs. Moretti stuff. I am Ma, from here on out. You're about to marry my boy."

Arleen grabbed Najah in another bear hug, rocking her back and forth.

"Ma, let the girl breathe. You're gonna suffocate her with love."

"Oh, you!" Arleen released Najah and drew Tomasso into her arms. This broad, six-four man that looked like he could crush coconuts in his bare hands, turned into a goofy mama's boy right before Najah's eyes. It was sweet how he loved his mother, and it made Tomasso that much more attractive.

Najah hadn't grown up with much family. Her mom died when she was young. Her grandmother and father had raised her. Three years ago, she'd lost him to a heart attack. Heartbroken over his death, a year later, her grandmother went to sleep and never woke up.

Tiny as they were, they'd been a close little family. But now that they were gone, encountering Tomasso's big clan that was filled with cousins, aunts and uncles had always felt like the best kind of party you could ever get an invite to. She'd missed that.

"Come inside, you two. Dad's in the kitchen plating up the antipasto.

After an almost identical greeting from Ernesto Moretti, they sat around the table eating and drinking and eating some more.

"Now," Arleen said as she pushed back from the table. I can't believe you two kept your reconciliation a secret all this time. When did you two reconnect?"

Najah turned to Tomasso with wide eyes. In all their rush to get this scheme underway, they never discussed the particulars about how they came to be engaged.

"When I volunteered our vessel for the alumni cruise and realized Najah was going to be the event coordinator, I had to reach out and see if it was my Najah. And once we reconnected..." he placed his arm around her shoulders, pulling her into his side as he'd done so many times when they were kids.

And just like back then, Najah melted into him, inhaling deeply as the scent of him enveloped him.

"...It was like we'd never been apart," Najah finished.

She should feel bad for the lie she was sitting her telling this wonderful woman. But somehow, with all this nostalgia and familiarity surrounding her, it didn't feel as fake as it should.

This is not real, Najah. Don't get caught up in this fairytale.

Arleen looked over at the two of them with joy beaming off her, and Najah couldn't tell who was happier in this moment. Tomasso's mother over an engagement she believed was real, or Najah over an engagement she knew was fake.

Chapter 5

"I fixed up the pool house for you to give you some privacy. I'm sure you don't want the old folks hanging around all the time."

Tomasso didn't know what he'd done to deserve a mother who was this good to him, but he would pray the Rosary for the rest of his life to show his gratitude.

"Breakfast will be on the table by nine," Arleen continued. "...and Najah, you and I are going to nail down the details of the engagement party this weekend."

"Party what now?"

Tomasso struggled to keep his laughter inside as he watched Najah get swept up into the hurricane that was his lovely mother, Arleen.

"Najah, my oldest son has found a way to bring the only daughter-in-law I ever wanted back into this family. You know there's no way I could keep this information from the rest of the family."

"That," Tomasso interjected. "and once you told Aunt Rosie, everyone in the family was gonna know what happened anyway."

That earned him a wagging finger in his direction.

His mother loved him. There was no doubt in his mind about that. But seeing her like this, alight with joy and laughter because her son was bringing home "the one that got away", made his chest so full with a bittersweet ache.

He wanted this to be real. He needed to make this real. But if he'd told Najah that two days ago on the boat, there's no way she would've agreed to doing what he'd asked of her.

Seeing Najah like this, being drawn into his family like she always should've been, it was everything to him.

"See you kids in the morning."

His mother blew out of the pool house, finally leaving the two of them alone for the first time in hours.

"Tomasso, we can't let your mother throw us an engagement party."

Tomasso stepped into the one room pool house that had a platform bed in the far corner, and two short sofas creating the living room space. The kitchen was off to the side with an eat-in counter that completed the dwelling.

He threw his jacket on one of the couches and walked over to where Najah stood.

"Sweetness, you know how my mom is. Nothing has changed in all these years. Of course she's throwing us a party."

He could see the panic rising inside her. Her shoulders were drawn up and she was pacing.

"Tomasso—"

"Najah, stop." He walked over to her, placing his hands on her shoulders and pushing down, forcing her to relax.

"We agreed to do this for six months. Did you really think we'd never have to celebrate this engagement? You know my family?"

"Correction, knew," she interrupted. "I knew your family."

Those words burned inside of him. When they were together, Najah had spent more time at his house than she had her own.

"My family loved you, Najah because I loved you. Nothing has changed."

Najah pushed his hands off her shoulders and walked toward the large windows that displayed the in-ground pool in the back.

"That was fifteen years ago, Tomasso. I was an eighteen-year-old girl wrapped up in a boy who sold me a bill of goods about forever. That love doesn't exist anymore."

Silence filled the room as the angry rush of his blood pumped through his vessels. Tomasso had never been a hothead. Losing control wasn't his thing. But that didn't mean his anger didn't run deep.

And what Najah had just said pissed him the hell off.

Yes, he'd broken things off with her. He took full responsibility for it. He'd been a prick about how he'd gone about it, and he'd also taken responsibility for that too. But what he wouldn't do was allow her to shit on everything they'd shared. Not when he'd loved her so damn much. Not when his family had adored her as if she'd been born into it.

He stalked over to her, and as he did, she folded her arms, preparing herself for the next verbal barb she thought Tomasso would throw at her. But he was done talking. Najah needed to be shown the truth. And there was only one way to do that.

When he reached her, he snaked a hand around her neck, pulling her into him, slamming his mouth against hers.

The kiss was rough and punishing. It was intended to be. Not just for her, but for him too. He'd caused this distrust. He knew that. He'd hurt her. He'd known that too. But what she didn't know was in all that pain he was doling out; he'd served himself a healthy dose of it too.

He'd carried around that pain until it had become a dull ache that never ceased. And now, the cure to his pain was within reach but still so far away.

He would never recover completely until he had her back. All of her. Her heart, her soul, and her body.

But for right now, if he couldn't have all of her, he'd take the one part she was willing to give.

And she was definitely willing. Her eyes were focused on him, her breathing was heavy, putting those gorgeous tits of hers on display.

Her large nipples pebbled up beneath the white t-shirt she was wearing, and it took all of his control not to tear the fabric off of her.

She ripped her mouth away from his, dragging in one labored breath after another until she could speak. "This engagement is fake, Tomasso. We shouldn't do something we're only going to regret later."

He let a single finger slide down the soft angle of her jaw until it met the curve of her neck. Her breath hitched when he touched that spot that used to drive her crazy back in the day.

Then he was a little boy playing at being a man. Now he was a man who knew what the hell to do with a woman like Najah Temple.

His finger continued its journey until it was sliding across her collarbone, hovering just above her cleavage.

"Sweetness, I know I won't regret it." He buried his fingers into her curls, meeting her gaze head on. "What about you?"

She stared at him with half anger and all desire sparking in her eyes. He chuckled. She might be mad at him, but he'd wager she was just as mad at herself that she couldn't hide what she wanted.

And what she wanted was him.

From the way the tip of her tongue slide across her bottom lip, to the way her lids dropped halfway to closed, it was all there for the seeing.

"Answer me, Sweetness." He let his thumb slide across her bottom lip, dragging it oh so slowly from one side to the next. "If I stripped you naked and spread you across that bed up there and took my time tasting every inch of your skin, would you regret it?"

"Tomorrow," she whispered before she licked her tongue over his thumb, then closed her lips around it.

Instantly, his dick was hard enough to cut steel and he ached to stroke it just for a modicum of relief. He refused to move, though. To do so might change this moment they were in right now.

"I'll regret it tomorrow," she said as she stroked her hand across his straining erection that was trying its best to burst free of his jeans. "Tonight, I'm going to enjoy the hell out of this."

Chapter 6

S he was an idiot.

There was no other word to describe how utterly moronic the decision she'd made to let her guard down long enough to end up where she was right now.

And where was she?

In her ex's parents' pool house, lying buck ass naked in a bed, risking her self-respect for one moment of pleasure with the man who'd broken her heart.

Tomasso's heated gaze roamed down her size eighteen frame, setting every nerve ending she had ablaze.

Najah had always been a big girl, and her grandmother had raised her to love every inch of herself. There wasn't a person alive who could make Najah feel bad about the body she'd been born with. To her, every curve, every roll on her size eighteen body was beautiful.

That confidence was what had drawn the most popular boy in high school to her and kept him by her side for four years. And that same confidence had the older, sexier version of that boy staring at her like a starving man looking at a steak.

"Damn, Najah." Tomasso's voice was like gravel, rough against the air.

"You like it?"

"Like isn't a strong enough word." He pulled his shirt off, tossing it on the floor, before he knelt before her, pushing her knees open to make room for himself.

Before she could say another word, she felt the first lick of his long tongue against her slit, and it was absolute heaven.

"Fuck, Tomasso."

"I intend to, baby."

He spread her folds, feasting on her like she was his first, last, and favorite meal. And as greedy and needy as her pussy was, she wanted him to dine until they'd both had their fill.

He slid a finger inside her slick opening, and when she moaned in pleasure, he added another, stretching her, getting her ready for him.

She was almost there, almost ready to break apart for him.

"Tomasso, I need...I need."

"I know what you need, baby."

He stood up, bracing himself on one arm as he leaned along the length of her, sliding his fingers between her folds again, rubbing his fingers against her clit in a slow pattern, edging her closer and closer to the ledge.

And just when she was at the precipice, he slid three fingers inside of her, thrusting in and out, hitting that tender bundle of nerves that had her fisting the sheets, and calling his name.

He whispered in her ear, "Come for me, baby." And she splintered like distressed wood under pressure, her walls clamping down around his fingers as her orgasm seized her muscles.

He kept stroking her through her release, while his thumb rubbed against her clit, making the assault on her senses so much more intense.

When her climax finally ebbed, leaving her limp and ready to crawl up into a ball, Tomasso stood up, opened the flap of his jeans, and let the most beautiful erection fall free.

He took the hand dripping with her juices and smoothed it over his length.

The sight of him using her to get himself ready to give her more pleasure had her pussy aching and squeezing, needing to be filled.

He stepped away for a second, and when he returned, he had a foil packet in his hand.

Thank God he had the presence of mind to be sensible. Because the only thing she could think about was how much longer until she got to ride his pretty dick.

He sheathed himself then stood at the edge of the bed, pushing her knees apart as he lined himself up at her opening.

Inch by inch he slid into her. His fingers might have opened her up, but they in no way compensated for the sheer girth of this man's hard dick nearly splitting her open.

"Feels so fucking good, Najah."

He damn sure wasn't lying. This was better than good. This was sublime.

He pulled back, and she locked her ankles behind him, trying to keep him inside just a little bit longer.

"Your pussy is so damn greedy."

Again, he wasn't lying.

She slid her hand between them and rubbed her clit to take the edge off a bit, and he chose that moment to slam back into her, sparking the beginnings of what she was sure was going to be another fantastic release.

He rode her so fucking hard, his balls slapping against her ass, teasing the sensitive skin there between her cheeks.

It had been so long since she'd allowed anyone to touch her there. She'd had sex with other partners, but it never occurred to her to let them take her ass. She'd used her own fingers and toys whenever she got the urge, but no one had ever breached her rosebud except him.

He'd been her first in every way possible, and her body remembered. Now, it tingled in anticipation of his touch.

"I know what you want. Ass in the air, baby."

He separated their bodies, leaving her empty and wanting.

He didn't speak again, simply waited for her to do as he'd told her. She gathered what little strength she had and repositioned herself on all fours.

He slid his fingers inside her again. Pressing down on her g-spot from this new angle had her arms collapsing and her legs spreading wider to accommodate him, give him all the space he needed to move, and work, and pleasure her.

He quickly brought her to climax again before he slid back into her. His stroke was powerful and yet so sweet, it nearly brought her to tears.

"God you take me so good, baby. You're such a good girl."

She felt a slick finger circle her back entrance as he pumped inside of her pussy. He kept circling it there, adding increasing pressure against her rosebud until a fingertip breached her.

"You're not ready for more right now, baby."

She mewled beneath him. She was so close, all she needed was that extra push. Suddenly, the fingertip in her ass shifted and now his finger was fully seated inside her.

It was just a finger, but in conjunction with his dick stretching her pussy so wide, she was full to bursting, and without warning, her climax seized her as blinding pleasure took control of her.

And when she finally fell from that delicious peak he'd pushed her over, he removed his finger, grabbing a handful of each of her ass cheeks before he plowed into her until he found his own release.

He separated their bodies, going into the bathroom to dispense of the condom and clean up. He returned with a warm cloth, gently wiping away the evidence of the pleasure he'd gifted her with.

Pulling her into his arms, he gently cuddled her like she was a precious treasure he had to keep near and protect. When he covered them with blankets, she reminded herself that she'd regret this tomorrow. But tonight, she was gonna enthusiastically enjoy every orgasm this man could give her between now and then.

Chapter 7

"It's tomorrow, Sweetness."

Tomasso's fingers started their path down the soft skin of her abdomen until they were prodding her to open her legs wider for him.

"I know you had plans to regret everything we did last night."

His voice was a low grumble that dragged her from sleep and into a lusty haze.

"But I figure if I keep this pussy spread open and ready for me, you won't have time to regret anything."

At that moment, she let her legs fall open. Sure, she could've put up more resistance, but why should she. The way that man used his body to bring her to orgasm quickly and repeatedly was a marketable skill as far as she was concerned.

His fingers found their target, entering her slowly, so slowly she was already lifting her hips to try to get him to go deeper where she needed him to be.

"Are you sore?"

"In the best way," she murmured.

That earned her a nip on her neck, and a light pat against her labia.

"Turn over, I have a gift for you."

She didn't have to ask what it was. The way his voice dropped into its lower register when he said, "gift," made it abundantly clear just what type of prize he'd be rewarding her.

They'd crossed the line from heavy foreplay into full on sex when they were seventeen. And although they were young, they were always willing to try new things, to learn what they each liked.

Ass play had become a fast favorite for Tomasso. And because she trusted him so much, venturing into this uncharted area of love making felt safe.

The snick of a top being opened made her moan in her half wake, half sleep state, rubbing her mound into the mattress beneath her to get more friction where she needed it.

"You brought sex toys to your parents' house, Tomasso?"

"I sure as hell did," he chuckled as he gave her ass cheek a quick slap, followed by soothing touches to ease the sting.

"I wanted to bury myself balls deep in your ass last night, Sweetness. But I knew you weren't ready. Do you want me to get you ready?"

"Yes."

God she was a thirsty heifer. There had been no hesitation in her response at all. She'd take time to ruminate on that later. Right now, she just wanted the pleasure he was offering her.

He covered her back with his front, placing soft kisses against her shoulder, before he let something drop next to her pillow.

She opened her eyes to find three butt plugs of graduating sizes resting on the covers.

"Do I need to start small, or can you handle starting with the medium sized plug?"

He spoke in matter-of-fact terms. They were both grown and no matter how enthusiastic their play had been, he'd always taken care of her needs. The care he was showing her now, that was part of the entire seduction, part of the thing that made her want him even more.

She picked the moderately sized plug up and handed it to him. Cool liquid dripped onto her rosebud, and Tomasso massaged it in until his fingers were breaching her.

This time one finger became two, and short shallow strokes became deep until he was pressing her G-spot from the underside.

She came on a moan, her body shaking and trembling beneath his touch, and she relaxed just the slightest bit, and he gently pushed the tip of the plug into her.

It was slick, proof that he'd used a generous amount of lubricant. By the time she was halfway to her next orgasm, the plug was seated fully in her with the flared end holding it steadily in place.

"You're so beautiful like this, Sweetness. Spread out with my plug in your ass."

He helped her turn over before he picked up the condom. Soon, he was sliding his cock slowly inside her. She was being stretched everywhere, and it notched her arousal up even more, her pussy becoming so slick, that Tomasso was able to enter her easily.

After his first tentative stroke to test her limits, he didn't hold back, and she didn't want him too.

He pounded into her. His cock so deep in her pussy, and the plug in her ass, her body ready to shatter. It wasn't enough for him, though, her either.

He turned her over again, entering her again from behind. Once he was comfortably settled, he leaned down, pulling her upright onto her haunches as he drilled into her. A careful hand placed at the base of her throat while the other teased her clit, and her body was on sensation overload.

Her orgasm was too powerful, every nerve synapse firing at the same time from his multiple onslaughts. Her breath caught in her chest as bright sparks burst behind her closed lids as she drowned in a climax so powerful, it left her wet and limp against him, using his solid frame to keep her upright.

He laid her gently down on the mattress, holding himself over her and he looked down at her. "I want you to wear my plug all day."

She huffed, trying to catch her breath. "From what your mother said last night, it sounds like she plans to have me in boutiques all day."

"I know. But the thought of you fighting your own climax all day in public while that plug keeps you on the verge of release, my dick is hard just thinking about it."

He tapped the flared head of it with the tip of his cock.

"Do this for me, and I promise to make it all worth your while."

She moaned beneath him, wondering how she'd let herself be sucked into this. This was a fake engagement. They weren't a real couple. Not anymore. And yet, those lovely orgasms he'd given her were as real as every tangible thing in the room.

With him fucking the good sense out of her, all she could do was meet his steady gaze and nod.

"That's my good girl."

Chapter 8

"**Y**ou look fucking amazing."

Najah turned away from the mirror to see her fake fiancé staring at her from across the open room.

She wore a one-shouldered, mini body con dress that put all her curves on display. Between the rouching and her corset-like shapewear, the soft black material looked classy enough to wear to an engagement party and sexy enough to keep Tomasso's eyes pinned to her.

"You are trying to kill me with that dress. How am I supposed to do anything but watch you all night?"

She hoped her pointed brow revealed just how little she felt for him in this situation.

"Well, turnabout's fair play and all that."

He stepped closer to her, placing his hands carefully on her waist and the playful edge she thought she had begun to dissipate into the air.

She'd gone from feeling in control of their banter to out of control of herself, and that worried her.

She'd lost herself in this man once. She couldn't repeat that mistake again.

"Are you still wearing that pretty little accessory I gave you this morning?"

His words ghosted over her bare shoulder like fingertips. She wanted to lean into them. Everything about the way he teased her with his words to the way he'd owned her body last night was familiar, too familiar. That's exactly why she shouldn't give in. She just had to remember that.

"I am."

Tomasso's grin widened as his gaze narrowed. His stare so intense, he almost seemed to be looking through her.

"You have no idea how much I love it when you please me."

She shifted, and the plug pressed against her sensitive spot nearly forcing an indulgent moan from her lips. But she refused.

"I'm not doing it to please you. I'm doing it to please me."

Pleasing him had always been a mutually beneficial thing for her. Somehow, that knowledge didn't allow her to let go of the way she so desperately wanted to please him right now. It was childish of her. She knew that. But there was some little piece of her that wanted to hold back, even this tiny thing from him.

She had to hold back something for herself. Otherwise, she'd allow him to get too close and just like before, she'd end up hurt.

Not this time. Not ever again.

His eyes roamed over her, searching her features to see if there was anything more to her response. She schooled her features, trying to keep him out because the alternative wasn't something she could allow.

She stepped out of his embrace, leaning to pick up her clutch on the couch.

She looked up to still find him watching her from the same place she'd left him. This was a power struggle. They both knew it. But the difference was this was a game to him, something he was doing to get his kicks. And if she didn't remember that, she'd wind up worse than she was when he'd decided to leave before.

She had to win this battle. There was no other choice for her.

"We wouldn't want to keep your mother waiting. Coming?" Her tone was suggestive, and the wry lift of his mouth told her he hadn't missed her play on words.

He grabbed his suit jacket from the back of the sofa, hanging it over his arm.

"I certainly plan to."

***

"Ladies and gentlemen if I can have your attention for a moment."

Tomasso watched his father stand in front of the fireplace in the great room. That was always the place where all the big family announcements were made, so it didn't surprise him to see his dad standing there with his mother beaming proudly by his side.

His parents shared something special, something that he'd always wanted for himself. Without thinking, he placed his hand on the small of Najah's back, keeping her close to him.

He'd kept her close all night. Whether by touching her or watching her wherever she was in the room. And no, he wasn't being creepy. At least he wasn't trying to. He was just drawn to her energy.

"As a father, watching your kids meet their milestones in life...well, there's just nothing like it. Standing here tonight, watching my son,

Tomasso. get ready to take one of the biggest steps a man can take, it just does my heart proud."

There were celebratory noises made throughout the room, his family cheering him, cheering them, on.

"Najah, the day my son met you he came home with wide puppy dog eyes, and he said, 'Dad, I just met my future wife.'"

Everyone in the room laughed including Tomasso, because he remembered that conversation like it was yesterday.

"I thought it was just teenage hyperbole, but then he brought you home, and after watching the two of you together for four years, I knew my son was right."

Najah snaked her arm around his waist, and it steadied him, made him feel planted into the ground.

"When you meet the love of your life at fourteen, the likelihood is high that you'll have to go your separate ways so you can learn and grow. And when it came, it pained all of us. But just fifteen short years later..." The room erupted in laughter, and even Najah looked up at him, giving him a genuinely amused smile. "He brought you back home to us and we were overjoyed because you are our daughter, and this is where you belong."

The "here heres" and whistles filled the air as Ernesto lifted his champagne glass and waited for everyone else to follow suit.

"To Tomasso and Najah. No matter what trials life brings you, may you always find your way back to one another. May your love always be your North Star."

Fingertips tapped against glasses, signaling the crowd was waiting for the happy couple to kiss. He looked down at Najah and he saw something there, something genuine that he couldn't quite place. She wasn't acting, and neither was he. Could he dare allow hope to grow that maybe she was coming to trust him, if only a little.

"And since we're talking about beginnings. We have to come full circle and talk about endings too."

Najah's brow furrowed, not understanding what his father could be hinting at. But Tomasso had a good idea as he saw his father's business partners stand to his right side.

"I'd like to announce my retirement from the Triple M. And my wedding gift to my son once he's married, is that I am naming him as my successor."

The tightness in Tomasso's chest lessened. His father had done it. Hell, he and Najah had done it. This plan had finally come together, and they'd managed to save his father's legacy.

But the straight and harsh lines of Najah's face told him the celebration was indeed over. Once she uttered the most dreaded words a man could ever hear, telling him, "We need to talk." He was absolutely certain the party was done.

***

"Did he say he's not turning the company over to you until we're married? Because that's what it sounded like."

Tomasso closed the door to the study, walking her further inside the dark room before he replied. Though there were no lights on in the room, the moonlight and stars from the balcony bathed her in an ethereal glow that made him want to draw her near.

One glance at her brooked that thought. Her arms crossed and her body ramrod straight, this was a woman who wanted answers and she wanted them right now.

"My father knew we were faking our engagement."

She opened her mouth, but he put up his hands because he could see the question already in her eyes. "My mother doesn't know, just Dad. And if he did agree to this, it tells me his partners insisted on that stipulation, Najah."

She shook her head and then spoke through clenched teeth. "We can't get married. This engagement is fake. Or did you forget that?"

"Najah—"

"Tomasso, it's not real. You told me six months of pretending to be your fiancée, not your wife. We can't do this."

"I'm afraid we'll have to. It's the only way for this to work."

"It's not real, Tomasso."

"But it could be if you let it." He stepped closer to her, making sure her sight was filled with nothing but him. "Last night was proof, baby."

She closed her eyes tightly, wrapping her arms around herself. "The only thing last night was proof of was that we're physically compatible."

"You keep telling yourself that, Najah. But the way you came apart for me, that had nothing to do with physicality and everything to do with what's in here."

He placed a gentle hand against her chest, noting how her heart thudded strong and fast against it.

"We just work together, Najah. We always have, always will."

***

It all happened so quickly. One moment, she was panicked and ready to bolt, and the next, she was bent over the arm of a leather couch, riding Tomasso's face and screaming into brocade decorative pillows.

When she peaked for the second, no...maybe third time, he slid from between her legs, grabbing a condom and a travel lube packet from his wallet.

The plug was still there, a constant reminder of how on edge she was, how ready she was for what came next.

He was sheathed, leaning over her, he placed a firm hand on the back of her neck, pressing her into the cushioned arm of the sofa.

"This will always be real to me, Najah. And I'm not just talking about the sex."

She could feel the slow tug of the plug leaving her body. When it was fully removed, her body ached to be filled again.

The cool drop of lube onto her back entrance sent a jolt of excitement through her when it touched her heated skin.

He placed his cock between her ass cheeks, sliding back and forth, teasing her rosebud as she tried to guide him inside of her. But he wouldn't have it. He wouldn't let her have what she wanted so easily.

He leaned down, placing his mouth next to the shell of her ear before speaking.

"This is real to me, Najah. And I need it to be just as real for you."

He grazed his teeth against her earlobe as he slowly entered her. Her body's natural reaction was to brace.

"Relax, baby," he whispered. "Relax and let me in."

She did what he instructed, making her body relax when all her muscles wanted to do was tense up in pleasure.

But she stilled herself, letting him rock against her until the lube at her entrance and on his cock eased his way.

Finally, finally, he was balls deep inside her and the ache was replaced with sweet satisfaction.

With one of his hands on her hip, and the other caressing the weight of her breast, she was halfway to coming again.

Each stroke brought her closer and when his free hand slipped from her hip and reached around, finding her needy clit, she was ready to let go of all the tension, all her worries about this stupid plan of his, and most of all, all the pain that she'd held onto where Tomasso was concerned.

How could he make her feel this good when he was the one who made her hurt so bad?

It didn't make sense, and it frustrated her that she couldn't make it make sense. Something she was trying hard to ignore in this moment.

He changed his angle and thrust harder, making her entire body succumb to his will.

"You belong to me. Body, soul, and mind, baby."

He deepened his strokes, melding her emotions, hopes, and fears all into one. She didn't know if she could trust anything going on in her head right now. The only thing that made sense was the way her body responded to him, the way he answered every need instinctively. It had to be meant to be, right?

What little brain power she could muster disappeared when her climax crested, pulling her underneath into oblivion. And just before her last conscious thought, she heard him tell her, "You belong here with me in my world." Just before he cried out in his own release.

Chapter 9

Tomasso woke in the study and instantly knew something was wrong. Najah's luscious warmth was gone.

"Fuck."

She'd bolted. He'd known he was taking a chance asking her to make things real last night. She was skittish about his father's announcement. Understandably so. But damn, he'd thought she'd at least try to talk things out before she walked away.

He tugged his fingers roughly through his dark strands, needing the bite of pain to wake himself completely. When he sat up and looked around, he caught sight of the engagement ring that he'd slid on her finger only days ago.

Off her finger, it looked like toy, a worthless piece of glass. It was only Najah's beauty that gave that ring any kind of brilliance.

He pulled on his pants and his shirt, then plucked the ring from its resting place before looking at it long and hard.

"You can run, Najah. But I'll always catch you."

And with that, he made his way to the pool house where he could shower, pack, and leave to go get his woman.

***

Najah had stopped off at her office, trying to work herself into exhaustion so that all she'd have energy for was to fall flat on her face onto her bed. But the exhaustion that dogged her as she crossed the threshold of her Canarsie home was more than physical tiredness. It was the residual ache of knowing what she'd left behind.

She'd left Tomasso sleeping with nothing but a throw blanket covering him. If she'd called into Messy Mandy's podcast and revealed that tidbit of information, Mandy would've laughed her off the air. "Girl your fool behind left a fine-ass man with with a big dick, who sexes like a god, naked and alone on a couch? Honey, what is wrong with you?"

What indeed, Mandy? What indeed?

She stepped inside her foyer, kicking her shoes off her tired feet. She dropped her bag on the foyer table and headed toward the stairs to get to her bedroom when she heard, "You left me naked on a sofa in my parents' den, Sweetness. I'm kinda gonna need an explanation for that."

The sound of an unannounced person in her home should've brought fear. But her stupid mind couldn't seem to apply those sorts of fight or flight mechanisms where Tomasso was concerned.

"How did you get in here?"

He raised his brow as if she should already know the answer to that question.

"I know we spent most of our time at my house as kids. But you do realize that I did spend quite a bit of time over here with you and your family too, right?'

Her confusion must've still registered because he rose from her couch in the living room and walked to where she stood at the bottom of the stairs.

"Apparently you haven't changed the locks since the last time I was here, and you still keep a spare key under the decorative rocks near the back door."

"Note to self," she muttered. "Change the locks and find a new hiding place for the spare key."

He smiled, and the knot in her chest that she'd been carrying around since she'd walked away from him that morning slowly unraveled.

"I asked you to allow us to be real last night and you walked away. Explain what's going on to me?"

Although his voice was soft and non-threatening, she could see the intensity burning in his eyes. He not only wanted an answer, he expected one.

"Listen, Tomasso. I know I didn't fulfill my end of the contract, and I want you to know I don't expect you to deliver on anything you promised me as a result."

His gaze was hard and unyielding. He wanted her to feel its heavy weight.

"You think I'm here because I give a damn about some verbal contract we had?"

"Are you?"

The muscle at the corner of his jaw ticked as he moved closer to her.

"He lifted his hand toward her cheek and once his skin made contact against hers, he mellowed. The tension bleeding out of him as he looked down at her.

"I'm here because I want my heart back, Sweetness. You took it when you left me."

She saw real hurt etched into the lines of his face, and it pissed her off.

"Well, since you not only took my heart when you left me, but threw it on the ground and stomped on it right in front of me, I'd say I'm still ahead in this broken heart game."

"Najah—"

She pulled away from him. "No. No, Tomasso. You don't get to tell me about your broken heart when you intentionally destroyed mine."

His eyes widened and his jaw tightened. He was surprised and pissed about her refusal of him. Good. She was sick of him ignoring their history to make their past easier to swallow.

"I was a poor kid on scholarship at that preppy ass school for rich kids. For four years I took the abuse of your fellow entitled classmates. I took the mean pranks, the whispers, and the taunting laughter as I walked down the halls."

He took a breath to speak, but she held up her hand. "Yes, your buddies minded their p's and q's when you were present. But you couldn't be with me every single moment of every day I spent in that hell hole."

She pulled a hand down her face, turning around before she removed her jacket, hanging it on the banister before sitting on the bottom step.

"As terrible as the hazing was, I never let those people touch me. What they said couldn't hurt me because I knew who I was and why I was there. And knowing that my boyfriend...my best friend knew me and loved me too, nothing they could've said would ever have mattered."

Her eyes began to burn, and she could feel the unshed tears trying to spill, but she refused. She wouldn't give him the satisfaction.

"And that's why when you were accepted into your dream school all the way on the West Coast, I didn't think twice about turning down the acceptances and scholarships I'd earned to follow you across the country. You, the boy who'd loved and respected me on sight. You, the boy who'd done all he could to protect me from my tormentors. You, the boy who'd stolen my heart. And then two days after graduation, you, the boy who had my heart and devotion, you broke up with me, and told me it was because I didn't fit into your world. That we were too different. That I was too different."

She trembled from the memory of that day and the quaking allowed fissures in the emotional fortress she'd spent years fortifying. And this time when she tried to fight the tears, she couldn't.

They poured hot and fast down her face. While she could see his body poised to try to comfort her, he refrained, and she was grateful. Because when he touched her, she lost sight of reality, of the way things were. She only focused on how good he made her feel in the moment.

"It didn't matter when those other kids said I didn't belong, Tomasso. But when you said it, it mattered more than anything else in the world."

She wiped her face, but the tears kept coming, and she didn't know how she would ever make them stop.

"I can't just forgive and forget and allow us to be real again, Tomasso. No matter how badly I want to. Not when you cut me so deeply."

He stepped in front her, kneeling so that they were eye to eye. Sadness and what looked like remorse cloaked him. Whatever he was about to say, she knew he really meant it. Yet, she still couldn't see how any words could change what was between them.

"A week before graduation, you went out shopping after school with your grandmother, and I came home to find your dad and my parents sitting in the living room waiting for me."

He placed his hands over hers, and at first, she thought it was to calm her. But when she felt trembling in his hands, she wagered the reassurance was for himself.

"They told me they love us and loved us together, but we were too young to make the kind of commitment we were headed for. You were giving up everything to follow me to the West Coast, and I was gonna let you because I wanted you with me. But they pointed out that the scholarships you were being offered on the East Coast would make a life-changing difference in your world. That I had a million and one opportunities in front of me because I came from money. This was your only shot."

Najah thought back to that day. She was so happy about graduating and over the moon fantasizing about her and Tomasso's future together.

"I didn't want to listen, Najah. But eventually, I realized that they were right. That night, I promised your father that I would end things, that I would give you the chance to build your identity and your career without the influence of our relationship hanging over you. And so, I told you those terrible things..."

"Because you knew those words were the only ones that would hurt me enough to make me hate you, to make me walk away."

She raised her hands to his face, cupping his cheeks, needing to see him, to feel him. How had she not seen it then. She wanted to be angry with him, to hold on to the hardness that she'd carried for so long. But there was only one problem. She remembered how their love bordered on obsession.

She knew no one could've convinced her that they needed time apart to grow as individuals. Which meant she also knew that she understood how in his teenage mind, using the words of her tormentors would've been the only way to get her to walk away and live.

"Baby, I'm so sorry. But the truth is, when I saw you on that boat, I knew that everything our parents had said to me was true, and that my breaking up with you was the right thing to do."

He placed his forehead against hers and she could feel the tangible connection between them re-weaving and stitching itself back together. Only this time, with adult hearts and minds that understood how life worked, that bond was fortified, stronger than it ever was before.

"I have never stopped loving you, Najah. If you just give me a chance to show you, I promise you won't regret it. Just let me make us real again, please."

"Tomasso," she pulled back just enough to meet his gaze. "We were real again the moment I let you touch me. That's why I ran. I thought I could spend a couple of nights in your bed and walk away after the agreement was finished. But being with you, being with your family again...we were us. I knew if I stayed, if I kept up this farce of an engagement for six months, I'd be in too deep to walk away with my heart intact. I just couldn't bear the thought of losing you, of you hurting me again."

He placed a light kiss on her mouth. It was his way of trying to soothe the raw aches in both their hearts.

"If you give me a second chance, I will never hurt you like that again. Never."

"I know you won't," The burden of pain that had dogged her for so long crumbled, leaving her heart light and bringing a smile to her face. "Just like I know the truth is just as simple as this, Tomasso: You are mine and I am yours. Always have been, always will be."

"Does that mean you will wear my ring again?"

"Only if we spend the next six months getting to know each other again and rebuilding our fortress around our love."

"That," he pressed a hard, passionate kiss against her lips, "is a promise I can definitely keep."

She buried her fingers in his hair, bringing his lips back to hers again, drinking from him so desperately as she tried to quench her thirst for him.

"Now bring your ring and yourself upstairs so we can continue to renegotiate the terms of this updated contract."

"God, in all my years of business," he sighed. "the words 'renegotiate, terms, and contract' have never made my dick so hard in my life."

She stood up, and he followed suit.

"I guess that means you'd better follow me to my room quick, fast, and in a hurry."

He shook his head. "No ma'am. Not when I have a better idea."

He palmed her ass, and before she knew what he was doing, he lifted her off the stairs, forcing her to lock her legs around him as he climbed each step. And when they entered her bedroom in record time, and he was peeling her clothes off her before she could say yes, please, and thank you, she wholeheartedly agreed his idea was in fact better.

This was who they always were together, how they should always be. Now that they'd found their way back into each other's lives, Najah wouldn't let anything, or anyone tear them apart again.

Epilogue

One year later...

"Tomasso," she let her hands drop down to his forearms as she stepped out of his embrace. "I need to get back to work."

With a smug smirk, he stepped into personal space again.

"You can't run from me, Sweetness. We're on a boat surrounded by water."

He did have a point. They'd be at sea for the next two days until they returned to port.

"Have dinner with me tonight, Sweetness."

"And if I don't?"

The corner of his mouth hitched up as he ran a careful hand over his beard.

"Well, if you don't come to me, I'll be forced to come to you. And I doubt you'll get much work done with me underfoot."

A quick glance around the room and she could see the attendees slowly entering the event space. She'd landed the annual contract with their alma mater. But if she wanted to keep it, she had to always bring her best work. And anytime she stood for more than five minutes in this man's presence, giving her attention to anything else was almost impossible. Distractions and work didn't mix.

And her husband, Tomasso, with his big muscles and irreverent smile was one hell of a distraction she couldn't resist.

"Fine," she replied. "I'll have dinner with you."

***

"You've dragged me up here," she muttered, leaning against the door, making her hip jut out. "I hope you have a reason for it."

"A reason? Yeah, I've got a few of those."

He pulled her into the room, securing the lock on the door as soon as it closed.

"The first," he said, pulling her into his arms and kissing her deeply until they both had to tear their mouths away for air. "I always have dinner with my wife."

They'd made that deal when his dad started handing more responsibilities over to him at work. His work days were longer, and after one too many nights of coming home late and finding Najah asleep, he'd instituted this rule.

Whether they ate together in person or via Zoom, they always took time to share the last meal of the day so they could check in with each other and keep their connection strong.

"Two," he began again, "you work too hard, and I need to make sure that you're stopping to take care of yourself."

Najah was a workaholic who if not stopped, would work herself sick. She'd get dehydrated, fatigued, and then all of a sudden, she'd come down with a terrible cold because she'd worn her resistance down. He was her husband now, it was his job to protect her, even from herself.

"Are those the only reasons you wanted me up here in your suite?"

She snaked her arms around his neck, keeping his mouth close to hers, just like they both liked it.

He wrapped his arms around his waist, sliding his hands down to smack her glorious ass as he ground against her.

"Three," he tugged his bottom lip between his teeth and then smiled. "You left me with a hard dick this morning. I've been dying to bury myself in that beautiful ass of yours all day."

"Awww," she cooed. "Poor baby. We can't possibly have that."

She pushed his suit jacket off his shoulders, then made quick work of removing his tie, and then dress shirt. Next, she undid his buckle and opened the placket of his slacks.

Soon, her warm hand enclosed his hard length. She gave him a teasing stroke. And just as he began to moan in pleasure, she stopped stroking and led him to the large bed in the middle of the luxury cabin.

She stripped him of every remaining piece of clothing he wore and motioned for him to sit on the edge of the bed.

As soon as the backs of his thighs touched the cool sheets, Najah was on her knees, opening that sexy mouth of hers, taking him into her heat.

He braced himself on his elbows letting his head fall back as she cupped his balls and began lave his length with her tongue.

As much as he loved burying himself in her ass and pussy, having her take him into her mouth was the quickest way to get him to release. It was too hot and that fucking tongue of hers was too damn talented for her own good.

And she knew it too.

That's why her smug ass was looking up at him, smiling as she licked his balls. She thought she had the upper hand. At the moment, she did. But her victory would be short lived. Tomasso came prepared, and he wasn't above playing dirty in their sex games.

She was sucking him earnestly now, caving those beautiful high cheeks as she increased the suction. If he allowed her to keep this up, it would be over all too soon. He couldn't have that.

Before the sensation could become too much, he removed himself from her mouth, taking her chin between his thumb and forefinger, lifting her mouth to his.

He drank from her and when she opened her mouth on a tantalizing moan, he plunged his tongue inside.

He broke the kiss, instructing her to strip while he went to the nightstand drawer to get what they needed.

Tomasso wanted Najah any day that ended in a "y". That was given. But when she'd scurried out of their bed because she was running late for work, leaving his only option for release being his own hand, he'd plotted on how best to make her pay for it.

His answer was so wicked, he smiled as he watched her walk toward him,

"This is gonna be fast and dirty, Sweetness. You okay with that?"

She cupped her breasts and tweaked her nipples in response, and he thanked his lucky stars yet again that this woman was his wife.

"Assume the position, then."

She did as instructed and he dropped her Rose vibrator, a condom, and a bottle of lube on the bed. He loved this damn toy. The suction and vibration of the Rose on Najah's clit made her shatter every time. But this particular version of the toy had a dildo attachment that would allow her pussy to be full while her clit was stimulated, leaving her ass the only thing left to fill.

He coated both ends of the toy with a generous amount of lubricant, then sheathed himself and lubed his condom covered cock.

With her head down and ass in the air, she made a damn pretty sight. He slowly inserted the dildo inside her pussy and smiled as she moaned in satisfaction.

"You like that, Sweetness?"

She moaned again as he slid it out and re-inserted it.

"You know I do."

He sure as hell did. Not just from the sounds she was making, but the way she clamped down on the toy every time he tried to pull it out.

He pressed the power button on the bulb side of the toy, placing it into the eager hand she'd slid between her legs.

"Work yourself, baby. But don't come."

He saw the pout as she turned her face to the side on the pillow.

"God, you're a bastard."

He certainly was, but they both knew she'd thank him for it in the end.

As her body began to tremble from the double stimulation, Tomasso ran his fingers of the jeweled end of her new butt plug. Every time her hips shifted and jerked, this way and that, that pretty gem winked at him, playing peekaboo between her ass cheeks.

He could come just from watching this. Hell, he had come just from watching this, too many times to count. But tonight, he wanted to be balls deep inside her when he succumbed to release.

He slowly removed the plug, loving the mewling sound she made as he did. Then he placed a firm hand on one hip, holding her in place while he carefully slipped his cock inside her.

Najah keened in pleasure once he began to move.

"Damn, Tomasso," was all she could mutter before he started moving in earnest. Soon, his strokes were deep and fierce. Their skin clapping together in conjunction with the obscenely slick sound of his cock moving in and out of her ass, made for a tantalizing melody that drove him to drill harder and faster inside of her.

"Fuck yeah, that's my spot!"

She yelled and he kept his hips pistoning there, abrading the sensitive flesh until she tensed, crying out his name over and over until she nearly went limp beneath him.

His balls were drawn up tight in his sac and his muscles were on fire as he kept up his punishing pace, stroking her until he pulled another screaming climax from her. Then and only then did he finally allow his body to let go, grabbing his own satisfaction.

His cock pulsed inside her with each spasm of his release filling the condom. He was soaring and his body, heart, and soul were free falling over the peak of his climax.

He eased out of her, going to the bathroom to clean himself up and returned to do the same for her.

After tending to her, he drew her into his arms, kissing her as he counted his blessings. Fifteen years ago, he'd done the hardest thing in the world and sacrificed their love to give her the chance to grow on her own. And now his ability to hold her, make love to her, and have her be the keeper of his heart, this was his well-earned reward.

"God, I love you, woman."

Half asleep, she chuckled as she snuggled closer to him.

"You only say that because I fuck you senselessly."

He tightened his hold on her as he kissed the back of her neck.

"Technically, that is true. However, it's not the only reason I love you, Najah."

She turned around his arms, facing him with a satisfied smile on her face.

"Then what's the other reason?"

"Because I can't breathe without you. You're everything to me."

Love shone in her dark brown eyes, making the image of the moon-lit ocean outside their window pale in comparison.

"Well," he said as he gave her ass a loud smack, gripping a handful as he drew her closer to him. "That, and the fact that your ass play is unmatched."

"You are incorrigible," she teased.

He pointed to himself. "I am an ass man. And you love me for it."

Najah laughed aloud, the happy sound drawing laughter from him too.

When she could catch her breath and speak again, she looked up at him with love etched into every feature, every line of her body, and said, "You sure as hell got that right."

The End

About The Author

LaQuette writes sexy, stylish, and sensational romance. That means sentimental & steamy stories (Hallmark-like tales with lots of sex) with big emotions featuring fashionable & savvy characters.

This Brooklyn native writes unapologetically bold, character-driven stories. Her novels feature diverse ensemble casts who are confident in their right to appear on the page.

If she's not writing, she's probably trying on or looking for her next great makeup find. Contact her at https://dot.cards/laquette. Browse her books at laquette.com/books.

Bedding The Enemy

Available at Amazon

Blurb

Masaki Yamaguchi has lived by one rule: Bend the world to your will, and break those that refuse to comply. This motto has served him well as the head of the Yakuza family in Canarsie, Brooklyn. However, when he meets a soulful beauty with locs from Brownsville with her own set of rules, things aren't as clear, or easy as they used to be.

Oshun Sampson has worked hard to clean up her beloved Brownsville, Brooklyn. She's sacrificed everything, including her own happiness, for the cause. She'll be damned if she allows anyone the chance to destroy the progress she and her community have made. With the looming threat of the Canarsie Yakuza family closing in, the sexy new patron with the captivating eyes is a dangerous distraction she can't afford.

Two powerful leaders with one distinct line drawn between them. Will their passion be enough to hold them together? Or, will bedding the enemy result in a bloody war that tears them and their communities apart?

First appearing as a snippet in the Breaking Bad: 14 Tales of Lawless Love box set, Bedding The Enemy has been expanded to a 40,000-word novella. If quick, dirty, and intense reads are your thing, Bedding The Enemy is the novella for you.

Chapter 1

"Yesssss Masssss," Oshun Sampson moaned, as the man above her slid his cock inside her just the right way. Her pussy walls contracted, trying their best to strangle the length of him, keeping him planted inside her, rubbing so deliciously over her G-spot.

She couldn't remember how many times he'd made her cream all over him since they'd started this round. All she knew was she could feel her next orgasm clawing at her again. Her pussy lips so slick and swollen, each stroke making them sizzle with electricity.

"Let me watch you touch yourself while I fuck you," he whispered against her lips, as he bent down to steal a kiss.

She couldn't see him behind her closed lids. She'd given up trying to keep them open; her mind so blitzed-out from the way he was stroking her. But she knew his cocky ass had that crooked smile he always wore when he knew he had her at his mercy. It was a given anytime he had his dick inside her, or had her calling on the gods and goddesses as she came, that she was in fact at his mercy.

She fought the impulse to give in to him. It wasn't in her nature to submit to someone else's will. Oshun wasn't the kind of woman to let anyone control her. Control was always hers to wield. But, a one-night stand with a club hook-up three months ago changed all that. Now, instead of hitting it and quitting it the way she'd intended, she was laying in his bed, legs spread, pussy dripping, and hungry for his cock.

He slowed down his strokes as he bent down to kiss her again. "I know you heard me. Play with my pretty pussy and I'll let you come all over this dick again."

Her walls contracted at his promise, and a shudder spread throughout her body. As defiant as she wanted to be, she was too close and too hot not to acquiesce. She used her fingers to stroke herself slowly. Her clit was so sensitive it bordered on painful. She knew if she added too much pressure or speed, she'd tumble over into bliss.

She knew it would feel so good. But, she held back because it turned him on to watch her stroke herself. She ran her fingers from clit to slit. Her fingertips scraped against his cock every time he pushed in and pulled out. When she heard him hissing between his teeth, she knew his senses were overloaded as well.

"Faster," he commanded. "Don't fucking stop."

She sped up her motions. She could feel the familiar tension building up inside her, could feel the burning heat that seared her from the inside out. When the muscles in her thighs began twitching, and her pussy began contracting in powerful spasms, Oshun knew it wouldn't be long. Two more circular strokes and she felt herself break apart, felt her breath catch in her chest, and release spread like warm butter through her nerves.

The orgasm wrecked her, breaking her into unrecognizable pieces. Instead of helping her, Masaki Yamaguchi perpetuated her demise by slamming his cock over and over into her. It was hard and so rough, and she loved every minute of it. So much so, she begged him not to stop, begged him to keep destroying her.

He didn't disappoint. He kept hammering at her, prolonging the orgasm that ravaged her as she convulsed beneath him.

"God, you squeeze me so fucking tight, Oshun," he howled as his rhythm faltered. She felt his cock swell, and seconds later he pulsed his release into the latex barrier between them.

When he pulled out, she was still quivering, her body shaking of its own accord. Masaki must have seen her shaking as an invitation, because he rearranged himself so that his mouth met her pussy lips. His tongue gently bathed her, soothing and exciting at the same time. She'd thought he'd broken her, but within seconds, his tongue had her tensing in another release. This was sweet and gentle, but still, there he went again making her lose control.

He licked her cunt again, swirling it at her opening, groaning in satisfaction against her slick lips. He touched her once again with his tongue, finally relenting his hold over her when he heard her hiss.

Taking advantage of the reprieve she'd been given, she took a deep breath and opened her eyes. Dark eyes shining with mischief and a self-assured grin met hers. He took a moment to slowly pass that dangerous tongue of his over his lips, closing his eyes while a deep moan rumbled in his chest.

"God my pussy is so sweet."

As much as she wanted to disabuse him of the notion of him owning her sex, she knew she'd be lying. The way he kept her begging for his attention when they came together, there was no doubt in either of their minds that his fucking name was stamped across it in bright red letters.

Mas.

In every way that mattered, she certainly was. She didn't lie to herself about what and how deeply she felt for Masaki. What she felt wasn't the problem, how she lived was.

Being his was a notion she could only entertain while inside the confines of either of their homes. Here in his bed, or just a few minutes to the east in hers, she could wallow in the decadence of this man's affection, in the reckless abandon of her heart's greatest desire. But outside either of those situations, in front of the world, she could never take what she so desperately wanted; her place at his side as his woman.

He crawled up her body, pressing his mouth against hers, demanding that she open herself to him again. She barely parted her lips before his tongue was inside, painting her lips and tongue with the taste of her essence.

It was a heady experience, one that had her threading her hands through the ink-colored strands on his head, pulling him deeper into the kiss. If she weren't so fucked-out, this kiss could very well have been the start of another round for them.

She gentled the kiss, smoothing her hands carefully down his back until she met the meaty curve of his ass. She gave it a satisfying smack that pulled a wide grin from each of them.

"That never gets old," she said.

"What? You smacking my ass?"

Oshun chuckled. "That too. But I was referring to the way you fuck me until I'm boneless."

He placed a playful peck on the tip of her nose, and rolled over to the side, pulling her into the little spoon position. Dropping another peck on her shoulder, he snuggled in close behind her.

"I know a way to top me fucking you boneless," he offered.

"Not possible. No way you could improve upon perfection."

"Wanna bet?"

He rolled away from her, leaning toward the nightstand closest to him. When he reclaimed his position next to her, he handed her a square velvet box. The kind of velvet box that usually housed expensive jewelry. The thought of what could be inside this box had cold fear spilling inside her. It was only the lifetime of keeping her emotions buried from the rest of the world that allowed her to school her features.

Suppressing the shudder that threatened to spread through her, Oshun turned to Masaki, hoping the look of expectancy he wore didn't mean what she feared.

"What is this?"

"I believe in English, the word you're looking for is...gift. Typically, you have to open it to see what's inside."

Oshun sighed deeply and rolled her eyes.

"You know you're an asshole, right?"

He shrugged his shoulders and smiled. "I know you have a pretty little asshole that I plan on burying myself in once we've both recovered from our last round." He pointed to the still unopened box in her hand. "Stop stalling. Open it."

She felt the puckered skin of her rosebud contract at his words, and a slight pulse of electricity zipped through her clit. It didn't matter how he wanted to have sex with her, her body was always excited by his propositions.

Stay focused, Oshun. This isn't the time.

She opened the box, afraid of what it held, and was slightly relieved when she saw two keys resting on the cushioned bed instead of an engagement ring.

"I'm confused," she said with a shaky smile on her face. "What are these for?"

"They open my front door. This is my corny way of asking you to move in with me."

"Mas." The seriousness of her tone drained the light and easy atmosphere their lovemaking had created. She watched him tense up, pulling himself to a sitting position against the headboard.

"What, Oshun? You can save the "It's too soon" crap you're about to spew at me. We've spent nearly every day together over the last three months. You spend three to four nights a week sleeping in my bed, and the rest of the week I'm in yours. We already live together. All I'm asking is to make it official. So, if you're going to say no, at least don't insult my intelligence with a lie."

And there it was again, the one topic that always seemed to shake whatever peace they found in each other's presence. Oshun closed her eyes and pinched the bridge of her nose in frustration. It was fast becoming her conditioned response whenever Masaki brought up the topic of commitment.

"Mas, us spending nights together is totally different than us moving in together. I can't do that."

"You trying to tell me you're not there, you're not ready?"

She shook her head. Emotionally she was more than ready to make that commitment to him. Unfortunately, logic kept reminding her why it couldn't be. Her life wouldn't allow for the type of connection Mas seemed to be pushing toward more and more.

"Mas, you're so special to me. You know that. But, I've told you from the beginning I wasn't looking for a relationship. My life doesn't allow for it."

"What the fuck does that even mean, Oshun?"

He quickly swung his legs over the side of the bed, stalking to the dresser and rummaging for a pair of underwear inside. He stepped into a pair of black boxer briefs, and turned to her with his arms crossed against his chest. Standing there in the middle of the room, his full six-feet height seemed more ominous than usual.

The sharp slant of his eyes became more pronounced as his heavy gaze focused on her. His broad chest rose and fell in fast movements, his full-sleeve tattooed arms flexed with power, revealing carved, lean muscles. In that moment, she could see who he was so clearly. Asian, strong, powerful, confident, and sexy as all fucking hell.

"You're a waitress at a club, Oshun. Single, with no kids, or dependents that I know of. I mean, that's about the simplest life I can imagine. What the hell is really holding you back?"

She cringed at the harshness in his voice. She'd led him to believe her life was simple. He could never know otherwise. Keeping that in mind, she didn't hold the insult he'd just hurled at her against him. She knew it came from a place of frustration. He was frustrated she kept pulling away from him. But more importantly, he was frustrated about not being able to understand her reasoning.

She shifted in the bed, pulling herself up against the headboard, and covered her exposed body with the sheet. When they were naked, Masaki controlled the scene. That was a fact she'd accepted with much difficulty. Gearing up to have what could prove to be their biggest argument to date, she needed to maintain what little power she could.

"It's like you said, "that you know of." You don't know me, Masaki. And the truth is, I can't really afford to let you know me. I told you that night in the club I wasn't looking for forever. I wanted to have some fun, and that was all."

He ran his fingers angrily through the tapered dark waves on his head, then dropped his hands to the cut vee of his hips.

"Are you fucking someone else? Is that what this is about, keeping your options open?"

She shook her head, looking up toward the ceiling hoping for strength. Strength to keep her temper in check, strength to keep her emotions corralled, and strength to not give in to what they both wanted.

She pulled the covers off, and planted her feet firmly on the ground. She found her bra and panties strewn on the floor, and quickly pulled them on before sitting down on the bench at the foot of his bed.

"Masaki, as you've said, I spend three to four nights of every week with you, and you spend the rest with me at my place. Even if I wanted to fuck with someone else, when would I have time? I'm not seeing anyone else. I don't want anyone else. This isn't about you. This is about me and my life. It's about..."

The muffled ringing of her cellphone interrupted her her. She jumped up to get it, abandoning the conversation to answer the line.

She swiped right on the phone screen, and put it to her ear.

"Speak," she answered.

"We've got a problem. You're needed."

With no further response, she ended the call and grabbed her clothing scattered around the room.

"You are not leaving this conversation, Oshun. We are finishing this."

"It's already finished, Mas. I can't give you what you want. I can be with you, but I can't commit the way you want me to."

She dressed quickly, and walked down the stairs in her socked feet, grabbing her black low-top sneakers from the hall cupboard she'd placed them in when she'd arrived a few hours ago. She tied them, then turned to watch Masaki as he descended the stairs.

She didn't give him the chance to speak. She didn't have time for all that. By the sound of her partner's voice on the other end of her cellphone, things were about to get messy. But then again, things were always messy in her life.

That call served as a perfect reminder of why she could never commit to a man like Masaki Yamaguchi. Everything from the way he dressed, combed his hair, and even the way he furnished his house, denoted how organized and compartmentalized his life was. She wouldn't wreck his neat and clean life just to smear it with the grimy filth that plagued hers. Even though she knew he probably wouldn't agree, she cared too much to bring this baggage to his doorstep.

She kissed him quickly, then slipped through the door as she called over her shoulder, "I'll call you later today."

A chill spilled down her spine as she walked to her car, and thoughts of doubt began to plague her. "Hopefully he still answers when I call."

Chapter 2

Masaki slammed the front door and ran back up to his bedroom. He paced quickly back and forth across the large room, trying his best to quiet the rage bubbling in his head.

He'd tried hard to keep his other life away from Oshun, but Masaki couldn't allow himself to be pushed around by anyone, not even the soulful beauty who'd captivated him these last three months.

He knew he couldn't force Oshun to be with him if she didn't want to be, but he could damn sure get answers as to why. Answers he'd been seeking since he'd first connected with Oshun three months ago.

He could remember that first night so clearly in his mind. He'd seen the dread-locked vixen or rather he'd seen the dangerous way she'd swayed her hips to the vibrant dancehall rhythms blasting through the club's speakers. He watched the intricate sensual way she'd danced, and his cock chubbed up at first glance.

Not one to be driven by his desires, Masaki took notice, and set about securing her company for the evening. He'd watched her travel back to her seat at a booth in the VIP section once she'd finished dancing.

He'd stood at the bar, then asked the bartender to send her whatever she was drinking and put it on his tab. When she had the drink in hand, she held the glass up to him in salute, and motioned for him to come join her behind the velvet rope.

Sitting there talking to her had been an exercise in patience. He'd wanted nothing more than to find somewhere they could get naked for a few hours, there he could skeet off a nut or two and then be on his way. But, chatting for just those few minutes with the thirty-two-year-old young woman kept him enchanted long enough to remain seated next to her. Her chocolate brown eyes cued him into her keen wit, something even sexier than her cinnamon brown skin, high round tits, and ample ass.

They'd both known from that first drink they would end up fucking before the night was through. She'd been game with his plan, made no qualms about it, asked for no pretenses to be offered. She wanted to fuck, and she was all-in for allowing him to spend the night pleasing her. When they'd arrived at the hotel, she'd made it clear she wasn't looking for anything but some fun. She didn't want to exchange numbers, didn't want to know anything about him other than if he had enough condoms to last the night. Hearing her stipulations, he'd been certain he'd found the perfect companion for the evening.

It wasn't until the morning when he'd awoken to an empty bed, his dick damn-near raw from all the fucking they'd done, that he realized he'd made a terrible mistake. Letting that woman go without being able to contact her quickly became a regret he couldn't live with.

It had taken him a month of showing up at the club under the cover of having a good time to, "accidently" run into her again. She was serving customers drinks in the same VIP lounge he'd met her in. It didn't matter to him that she was a waitress. He wasn't interested in what she did for a living, only that she'd allow him to spend time with her. The memory of what it felt like to be buried so deeply inside her made him determined she wasn't getting away. He wouldn't relent until he'd convinced her a friends-with-benefits scenario was a workable way for them to enjoy each other and avoid the entanglements of being in a committed relationship.

He'd thought he was so smart in convincing her to go along with his plan. Too bad he hadn't calculated the fact he would become attached to more than just the sex, but to the woman as well.

Until this moment, they'd kept their lives separate, living in the now. But knowing she was holding back on him, especially when he suspected it was because of another man, didn't sit well with him.

If she wanted to run game, she'd chosen the wrong man to do it with. The power and connections he possessed always swayed things in Masaki's favor. Crossing him wasn't a smart thing to do. So, as much as he cared for her, if she wanted to act like a trick, he'd treat her like any other toy he'd possessed. He'd stake his claim, letting her and everyone else know there was a hefty penalty for touching what belonged to him.

He went looking for his phone when he heard it chirping on his nightstand. He picked it up, waiting for the caller to speak.

"Boss, we've got a problem."

Every time Masaki heard the word "Boss" his brain shifted gears, and the transformation began. Most days, Masaki wore the face of a clean cut real estate developer. He wore crisp button-down shirts, silk ties knotted to perfection with creased suits sharply tailored to fit only him. It was all a persona developed to prevent anyone who watched him too carefully from seeing the truth of who he really was; the head of the Canarsie Yakuza family.

Could this night fuck with my nerves anymore?

His second, Izumitani "Izzy" Hisato, was supposed to be in the middle of a high-priority job Mas had delegated to him. This call instantly pulled Mas from the day-to-day facade he wore for the public and Oshun, and made him sink into the ruthless gangster his organization demanded he be.

"Where are you?" Mas tucked the phone between his ear and shoulder, picking up the shorn clothes Oshun had pulled off him a few hours ago.

"Mother Gaston & Hegeman."

Masaki ran down the stairs and slipped his feet into his shoes.

"On my way now."

Masaki opened his door, and took the few steps to the driveway. A few moments ago, he was making love to his woman and asking her to move in with him. Knowing Oshun would balk at being called his woman, his mood soured more. Her skittish ass might be afraid of commitment, but he wasn't. She was his, and he was hers. In his mind, there was no other alternative than for them to be together. All that remained was for him to convince her of that.

But first, he had to deal with whatever this shit was that Izzy was calling him about.

"One problem at a time, Masaki," he whispered to himself. "One at a time."

***

Oshun shifted carefully through the massive crowd behind the NYFD barricade as she looked for one face in particular. At six-feet-two, Aesop Jenkins stood above most people in the crowd by at least a head. When she spotted his signature light Caesar haircut, cedar complexion, and the faithful toothpick he kept trapped between his full lips, she made her way toward him.

She said nothing when she found him. There were too many people around for her to express her thoughts openly. Not to mention, with all the emergency vehicles and their wailing sirens, there wasn't much chance of being heard anyway.

Her lips tightened into a flattened line as she squinted and assessed the blackened destruction of the now-extinguished fire. The row of attached two family houses on Mother Gaston Boulevard were now gaping holes of charred brick and steel. An entire block of buildings was gone in an instant.

She wasn't angry that AAM Developing had suffered such a loss. She knew by their track record those houses were going to be used as drug dens. But, on the other side of those houses were properties owned by members of her community. People she'd promised to protect if they followed her and adhered to the rules put forth by her council. Now those people would suffer along with AAM, and she couldn't have that.

"Club, now," was all she said before turning around to begin the two-block walk between the site of the fire and Heaven's Gate.

She didn't need to look behind her to know Aesop was following her. She didn't even need to hear the heavy footfalls of his workman's boots crunching hard against the concrete sidewalk. She knew he followed her, because it was his job to follow her, explicitly and implicitly.

She keyed in the alarm code and entered the doors of the darkened venue. Heaven's Gate usually brought calm to her restless soul. It was strange that a place usually filled with loud music and boisterous patrons dancing wall to wall could make her feel calm, but it did.

When she was just a club owner, her soul was at rest. It was rare when she didn't have to worry about making certain her community was protected from all threats, that her people were thriving in a system that set them up for failure from birth. But tonight, even inside these hallowed walls, there was no peace.

She headed for the basement, not surprised to see the lights were already on when she opened the door. She took purposeful steps down the staircase, and catalogued each face sitting at the rectangular table in the center of the room.

Big Craig, Chelly, and Uncle Pete ran the prostitution, the gambling, and chop shop rackets on the north side of Brownsville. Oshun controlled the money laundering and protection rings on the south side. With more money from her enterprise, and a larger piece of the territory under her control, Oshun sat at the head of the council. A fact that hadn't been easily accepted at first, especially by their eldest member, Uncle Pete. However, over time, they each saw her as a worthy leader who kept them paid, and paid people made happy subordinates.

Oshun taught them the way to remain successful was to engage community support. If they did things that placed the community at risk, they would always have to worry about some do-gooder trying to bring them down. They needed to take care of the community, and the community would take care of them.

The first thing she implemented was a community outreach of sorts. No crime was to be perpetrated against members of the community, only against entities that would take from the community. Her council members had to protect Brownsville, and they had to put an agreed-upon percentage of their profits back into the community.

Before Oshun instituted the restricting of how hustles were run in Brownsville, it was a wasteland of death, drug addiction, and crime.

Now, the community was beginning to thrive, and if it were up to Oshun, it would remain that way.

The key was organization. The community balked at prostitutes walking the streets, or women sacrificing their health as sex workers, and pimps beating and killing the girls they victimized. Oshun helped Big Craig set up brothels near the business district that only opened when the businesses closed for the day. All Big Craig's girls received regular healthcare at no cost to them, as well as took a favorable seventy-thirty split in earnings. Craig had balked about the changes in the beginning, but then the cops stopped busting his girls, and he saw his revenue increase rapidly. It was hard to argue with that logic.

When Chelly's gambling ring kept getting raided because nosey neighbors reported the undesirables hanging out on the block, Oshun formulated a plan. She turned Chelly's brick and mortar business into a virtual casino whose IP codes were damn near impossible to track. With the cost of overhead going down and the profits pouring in, Chelly happily conformed to Oshun's business model.

When legislation produced heftier penalties for grand theft auto, Oshun stepped in to help Uncle Pete restructure his hustle. Instead of stealing the cars himself, she had him contract out the work. She also had him taking on more insurance fraud cases than before. Stealing cars brought unwanted attention. Frankly, there were too many people who wanted to cash in on the insurance money when payments became too much to handle. So now, Pete didn't have to worry about breaking into and stealing cars himself. He simply designated a drop off spot with the owners, picked up the unwanted vehicles, and broke them down for parts.

Each one of her council members leveled-up when Oshun gave them a plan to run their businesses more efficiently, as well as in ways that didn't put them in opposition with the community.

Her plans always focused on minimizing risk and maximizing profit. The only thing the members had to sacrifice was violence and drugs.

It had been difficult to get them to give up their interests in guns and drugs. Getting them to police their people and penalize them for breaking council rules had been damn near impossible. But over time, these three learned times were good when they followed Oshun, and not so good when they went against her wishes.

Oshun quietly took her seat at the table, and waited for Aesop to close the door and take his place standing behind her seat.

"Someone want to tell me what happened?"

She watched the three council members gathered around the table, each directing their eyes to anywhere but where they needed to be, on her.

"Don't all speak at once," she said to the still-quiet room.

When no one spoke, she stood up, placing spread palms against the table as she braced herself. These three people had helped her bring Brownsville up out of the dark hardships that plagued communities of lower socioeconomic status.

No, it wasn't a wealthy haven overflowing with milk and honey. But, with hard work, Brownsville had become a working-class neighborhood. The council initiated programs geared to teach skills to the unemployed and undereducated. They'd sponsored grants designed to place competitive tools in their schools, and provided opportunities for residents to attend college, and start businesses within the community. They were doing good work. Brownsville was still on the come-up, but at least they were moving in the right direction. Tonight was the first time in her ten-year reign she worried all her work could be undone.

"What the fuck happened? As far as I understand it, the plan was for us to sneak in and fuck up their shit enough to cause code violations for the inspectors coming in a few days. How the fuck did we jump from that to burning down their fucking buildings, along with the neighboring houses owned by our damn people?"

Uncle Pete, an older man who was an original gangster from when her father was running Brownsville, finally turned his gaze to hers. He still wore wool fedoras or Bermuda hats wherever he went. He took a pull from the cigar resting between the thick pointer and ring finger of his right hand.

"It wasn't part of the plan, Oshun. Shelly, Craig, and me put some of our best people on the job. Aesop oversaw it all. Them damn Yakuza was waiting on them when they got there."

She turned to Aesop, her right hand, for confirmation of the old man's version of events.

"They ambushed us," Aesop said as he nodded his head. Just as we were finishing up, they caught us. There was a struggle between one of them and Craig's people while he was messing with the wiring. A light broke, and the fire started. We barely made it out alive."

She digested Aesop's comments, turning them over repeatedly in her mind. There was something picking at the back of her mind that didn't sit right with her. They'd watched this site for more than a month to get AAM's pattern down. They'd known everything about their security and had planned this job accordingly. Oshun wasn't sloppy, and she didn't allow her people to be either. Something was wrong here.

"How the fuck did they know we were coming?"

Again, everyone sitting at the table remained quiet.

"Someone talked," she answered her own question. "That's the only way they could've found out about our plan. Find out who the fuck is telling tales. We reconvene in two days. By then, y'all silent asses better have answers for me."

She stepped away from the table, walked up the stairs and out of the club. Her anger turned to breathtaking pain when she glanced at the burned ruins marking her failure to keep her promise to her people.

The sadness cloaking her soul weighed heavily on her, pulling her into a sinking pit of despair and disappointment as she stood there trying to figure out how she was going to fix this. The easy fix was to help her neighbors rebuild. That would take some of the burden off, but she knew it wouldn't repair the parts of their spirits that were destroyed with their mementoes, and memories that often colored the places a person called home.

"Oshun?"

She turned around at the familiar voice calling her name. It was out of place, somehow not fitting properly into her surroundings.

"Masaki? What are you doing here?"

It seemed like hours since she'd left him standing pissed off at his front door. A quick glance at her watch told her only forty-five minutes had elapsed. Did he follow her? Did he track her down to this site? She shook her head, trying to loosen the discomfort those thoughts brought to her.

He couldn't have followed you. You would've noticed a tail. But how and why was he here?

"One of my employees called to alert me of the fire. What about you?"

"I know many of the people who live in this area. I needed to come down and see how bad it was. Needed to see if there was any way I could help."

It wasn't a complete lie. It was mostly true. Yes, she did know the people who'd lost their homes. But Masaki didn't know about the true nature of her ties to the club. He didn't know she was the owner, and he damn sure didn't know about her connection to the underground council that, until tonight, protected Brownsville from all threats.

She replayed his words in her mind on a loop until something clicked in her head. "Did you say one of your employees called you?"

He nodded. "Yeah."

"Why would a real estate agent need to know about a fire that ravaged houses that weren't for sale?"

"Because my development company owns the properties on the other side where the fire began."

"You work at AAM Development?"

He shook his head. "No," he answered. "I own it."

Little more than an hour ago she was laying in his bed, quivering with need, falling victim to the pleasure he expertly doled out. Now, she was standing in the wake of the destruction she'd helped unleash on her own people. And worse yet, the man she'd been so captivated by for the last three months was part of what had led her down this dark path.

Dear God, I'm sleeping with the enemy.

Chapter 3

Oshun sat in front of her computer watching as each line of info she scrolled climbed up the screen. She wasn't the greatest hacker in the world, but she knew enough to get the information she was looking for.

Birth records, social security number, citizenship, educational documents, professional licenses, and property listings was some of the information she'd been able to get so far. Masaki Yamaguchi's life was spread out for her inspection on the large computer screen. Now, she just had to dissect it and piece it all together to make sense of the confusion in her head.

Everything was as Mas had told her. He was born in Tokyo, Japan, immigrated with his parents to the States when he was a toddler, spent his life living in Canarsie with his parents, and owned AAM Developing.

Oshun rubbed the side of her temple, trying to stave off the headache she could feel creeping up behind her eyes. This was outrageous. How could everything come back so clean if he was in bed with the Yakuza?

He lived in a simple two-family home in Canarsie, Brooklyn that he'd converted into a duplex. He was a product of public education. He wore a suit and tie to work every day. He was clean, maybe too clean.

She allowed memories of their union over the last three months to play in her head. Nothing about their time together pointed to anything screaming a Yakuza connection.

He doesn't even have full body tattoos.

She allowed her mind to conjure up the image of him naked. She took a deep breath to remind herself this wasn't about pleasure, this was about the survival of her organization and her community.

Tanned skin, smooth to the touch with very little body hair. His chest, was strong and carved, and his arms...

"Oh, my God! His arms."

She was right, he didn't have the extensive full-body tattoos Yakuza members were notorious for. However, he did have full-sleeve tattoos on each arm.

She pressed harder against her temple as she remembered a distinct conversation they'd had about his tats. The first night they'd slept together, she'd noticed them, noting how strange it was to find them on a man who looked so pristine. He'd laughed, telling her they were a result of rebellion against his father, and the life his father had planned for him.

It was a perfectly fitting answer; one she never questioned until this moment. Now that she knew he was the owner of AAM, she wasn't certain if Masaki's answer felt as true as it once had.

Dull vibrating against her desk pulled her eyes away from the computer and down to her phone. Masaki's name flashing across the screen made the bottom of her stomach twist into an uncomfortable knot. She slid her finger left, sending the call to voicemail.

She'd been ducking him since the fire. That was a week ago. A week of gaining access to government databases and sorting through all the information she'd procured, yet she still didn't have a definitive answer. Was Masaki involved with the Yakuza, or wasn't he?

Nothing in the documents presented a clear picture. Nothing definitively said, "Yes, I belong to an evil, criminal organization that is trying to destroy your community."

Determined to find what she was looking for, she delved back into the data on her screen, scouring it once again in hopes of either vindicating Masaki, or convicting him. This middle ground filled with uncertainty and doubt was an uncomfortable place she refused to dwell.

If Masaki was mixed up in the Yakuza, he'd go down with them. It wasn't a choice she wanted to have to make. In fact, she desperately wanted this all to be some crazy misunderstanding.

Though she'd never admit it to him, Masaki had become someone important to her. He wasn't just a fuckboy she'd picked up at the club. The truth was, even though that's what she'd told herself all the time, she'd been in denial about how strongly she felt for the man. She'd allowed herself to believe her only interest in him was the sex. The way her heart leapt when he'd asked her to move in completely destroyed any idea that their connection was only about their sex. Your heart didn't dance when an insignificant fuck buddy asked you to commit.

Sadness filled her as she pondered what all the latest developments meant for them. She'd known soon enough she would have to walk away. Him giving her keys to his place, asking her to move in, was the beginning of the end for them. But, even though she'd sensed the end approaching, she hadn't thought she might have to bring harm to

Masaki if they went their separate ways. A connection with the Yakuza meant there'd be no amicable parting. This would mean war, and war was always bloody.

A loud banging on the door made her jump to her feet and focus her attention toward the foyer. The sound repeated itself, making her reflexes kick into overdrive. She reached in the drawer of her desk to remove her pistol. She cocked it, and flipped the safety off.

The loud thumping kept rumbling against the door. She stepped quietly and carefully toward the sound. A brief peek at the security monitors on the nearby hall table showed an animated Masaki banging on her door with such force she could feel the vibrations through the floor.

Securing her gun behind her back, she called out through the door, "What do you want?"

"Open the door, Oshun! We need to talk."

She took a deep breath, hoping the added oxygen would force her brain to stop thinking of how tasty he looked in his tight black t-shirt. The fabric was stretched so tightly across his muscled chest, it was difficult to focus on how she was going to resolve this situation.

"Mas, today isn't a good day. I really need to be alone."

She anticipated more yelling to accompany the anger that had him pounding his fist against her door only moments before. What she received instead was soft-spoken concern that unnerved her more than the violent banging had.

"Oshun, I've been worried sick about you. The last I saw you was the night of the fire. You haven't answered one of my calls since then. Please, just talk to me, baby. Tell me what's wrong."

The sound of concern in his voice reminded her of how gentle he always was with her. He always sought to take care of her, meet her needs. It grieved her that her connection to the council had never allowed Oshun to reciprocate in kind.

"Watashi no megami, watashi ni hanashite kudasai."

God, this man knew her weaknesses. Her mind raced with so many tender moments they'd shared. They were all filled with him working beyond her rough exterior by sharing his heritage with her.

It seemed silly, him speaking to her in Japanese, or him making her traditional Japanese meals shouldn't have impacted her so greatly. But every time he did, it was as if he were sharing something so special about himself that she couldn't help but feel proud he'd chosen to expose himself to her.

In their three months together, he'd taught her enough Japanese that she could pick up parts in a conversation to understand general meaning. That phrase specifically, he'd used it consistently when he was attempting to get her to share herself with him.

My goddess, please talk to me.

She remembered the first time he'd spoken those words. She'd asked him why he'd referred to her as a goddess. His response, "I didn't call you 'a' goddess, but 'my' goddess. Mine because that's how I see you, and goddess because Oshun was an African goddess."

It shocked her that he'd known anything about the history of her name. It shocked her even more that he cared enough to learn it on his own without any prodding from her.

Hearing him appeal to the soft spot he knew she had for him made Oshun replace the safety on the gun, and slide it behind the security monitors on the table before she unlocked the door and opened it.

"Mas, calling me your goddess isn't going to fix this."

He walked past her, heading directly for her living room. If she'd been smart, he wouldn't even know what her living room looked like. But, she'd allowed herself to fall so deeply under his spell, she'd permitted him in her home within a month of them meeting. Now, he was comfortable enough in her place that he didn't need her to escort him to any part of it. Yet another mistake on her behalf she'd have to try to rectify.

"Oshun, you don't just get to forget about me. Not without some sort of explanation anyway."

His anger evident by the narrowed slits of his eyes and his squared shoulders held up by his hands positioned on either side of his waist. He was angry, but there was a control to his anger that made her reasonably certain he wasn't there to hurt her.

She shook her head quickly. A week ago, she wouldn't have thought it possible for Mas to hurt her. But, now that she knew there might be some connection between him and her enemies, she'd be a fool not to consider his ability to bring harm to her.

"I'm not sure what you want me to say, Mas. I told you when we started this I wasn't looking for anything serious. I'm sorry if the time we spent together made you think otherwise. Moving in together isn't something I can do."

He folded his arms across his chest, widened his stance, and licked his lips.

"So, you going ghost is all about the fact that I want you to be more than a piece of ass to me?"

She dropped her eyes to the floor as she nodded her head. Oshun knew full well she was more than just a sex partner to Masaki. He treasured her; it was evident in the way he expertly played her body with the simplest of touches. It was glaringly obvious in the ways he took care of her outside of bed, cooking for her, and showering her with attention and affection whenever they hid behind the walls of each other's homes.

He stepped closer to her, using his finger to lift her chin, ensuring her gaze was locked on him.

"You don't believe this bullshit you're spewing. You may not say it Oshun, but, we both know I wasn't the only one entangled in this thing between us."

He dug his fingers through her locks, pulling her mouth to his, slipping his tongue inside as soon as their lips met. His right hand moved deftly up the side of her hip and around her waist, pulling her abruptly against him.

She tried not to crumble, well, at least that's what she told herself in her head. But the truth was as soon as his lips touched hers, she was willing to do just about anything Masaki wanted.

He removed his hands from her hair and waist, moving them to the front of her button-down top. While his mouth still devoured hers, he pulled the top apart, letting his eager hands cup her lace-covered breasts. He ran his thumbs across her nipples, smiling against her mouth at the shiver he felt pass through her.

When his touch elicited a deep moan of satisfaction from her, he pulled his mouth away from hers. Securing his hands under her arms, he pulled her up until her legs were wrapped around his waist.

He walked them to her bedroom, laying her gently across the cool white linens beneath her. He pushed away from her, briefly taking the inviting warmth of his body with him as he reached for a condom in her nightstand drawer.

He didn't bother undressing them. He pulled his pants down far enough to pull out his thickening cock and sheath it. He lifted her skirt, and pushed her panties aside with two probing fingers, checking to see if she was ready for him.

The slide of his digits in and out made her walls weep and contract, begging to be filled with something meatier than the lone finger he was using.

She was too turned on to care about how desperate she looked with her legs spread, humping his fingers, begging him for more. Oshun slid her fingers between her lips, swirling them over her sensitized nub.

"You have no idea how much I love watching you touch yourself. How much it turns me the fuck on to watch you get yourself off."

Yes, she did. As much as she enjoyed masturbating on her own, watching his dark eyes sparkle with desire as he watched her pleasure herself made cumming by her own hand a favorite pastime.

He removed his fingers from her cunt, and waited for her to replace them with her own. She slid her hand under her thigh and inserted one finger inside. She was wet, slick with need, making the one finger slide effortlessly in and out of her. When the single digit wasn't enough, she added another and moaned at the electric sensation of being penetrated.

Fucking herself on two fingers of one hand while rubbing her swollen clit with the other had her passion cresting. She was about to fall over the edge just as he pulled her fingers out of her and slammed his cock into her.

The feel of his domed cap rubbing against her happy spot in perfect rhythm made her come apart. She could feel her muscles tightening with each squirt of her release. She couldn't worry about how soaked her sheets would be when they were done. The way he was fucking her, pulling each wave of her orgasm from her, her brain couldn't muster enough give a damn to worry about anything else other than how good she felt cumming on his cock.

When her legs were quivering from the last shocks of her orgasm, Masaki leaned over, pounding into her, wearing her slick walls out, pushing her over into another orgasm as he reached his own.

When his rhythm faltered, and she felt the swell of his cockhead inside her, she contracted her walls, milking him of his release, the way he'd taken hers.

When he was done, he leaned over, kissing her so sweetly it made her ache for more. He looked into her eyes, chest still heaving from their rigorous fucking, and his breath still a struggle to control.

"What we do," he gasped. "This isn't just about sex."

He pulled out, removed the condom and tossed it into the wastebasket beside the bed. He laid back down, pulling her into his arms, holding her head against his chest.

"Don't run from us, Oshun. Give me the chance to show you what we could be if we only tried."

Too tired and satiated to fight, she simply nodded her head, snuggling closer to him. She kept her eyes closed until his even breathing assured her he was asleep.

She untangled their limbs carefully, then set about removing her disheveled clothing, and pulled a long t-shirt from her closet. Once it was on, she quietly stepped out of the room, closing the door with a soft click. She picked up her cellphone from her desk, and walked out onto the balcony of her living room, closing the sliding door behind her.

Her second answered on the first ring. "What do you need?" Aesop's question was a loaded one. She needed the man in her bed to not be involved in the middle of this mess she'd found herself in. She needed to be able to care for him without dread looming over her head.

Unfortunately, she couldn't tell her friend that. Instead she decided to end this shit as quickly as possible. She'd sacrificed her life to the game. But for some reason, she wasn't inclined to sacrifice the connection she shared with Masaki so easily.

Call it love, call it lust, but whatever it was had a hold on her. Enough of a hold that she worried about their ability to survive the hell they'd find themselves in.

"Set up a meeting with the other side. The leader, 'Sop. He and I are gonna figure this shit out. I want this done. Brownsville almost burned to a crisp last week. We've gotta find some middle ground quick before there are more casualties."

"I'll get back to you when I have something in place."

She ended the call and took a deep breath. Brownsville couldn't suffer any more than it had. And maybe if she settled this shit, she could find a way to keep Masaki out of all of this. Maybe she could find a way to keep him in her life too.

Lies You Tell

Lies You TELL

ST. JARED'S MEMORIAL 1

LAQUETTE

Available at Amazon

Blurb

A mob boss finding his dead lover alive six years after her death? Shocking. Learning they've got a five-year-old son? Deadly.

Six years ago Sanai Ward fled her home in Florida when her lover's infidelity nearly brought her life to a fiery end. Devastated but determined to create a safe and happy life for the child she was carrying, Sanai started over from nothing. Single parenthood isn't easy. But the joys of watching her beloved Nazario thrive is more than enough motivation to ignore the ache in her heart for the man that shattered her soul.

Dante De Luca is a passionate man who's had his life stolen from him. Six years ago he was in love and happy, until his woman was killed in a fire. There was nothing left in the ashes but the locket he'd placed around her neck. Too angry to deal with his loss, Dante sought to make the world pay for his broken heart by forming an unholy covenant with an unspeakable ally. He'd live to regret it, but signing away his humanity to the devil seemed meaningless when his soul was already gone.

When an accident involving a family member draws Dante to New York, it forces an unexpected meeting between him and Sanai. Then Dante has to decide what's more important: his rage and revenge, or the safety of the woman he once loved and the health of his new-found son?

Chapter 1

S anai stood in front of the full-length mirror on the back of her en-suite bathroom door. She smoothed lotion over still shower-damp skin. First her toned thighs, then over her flat stomach and continued the passage of her hands down over the deep curve of her hips. She rubbed her skin lovingly as she continued up her arms, over the firm swell of her breasts, onto her strong shoulders, and eventually her face. She was diligent in keeping her movements steady, forcing her limbs to work despite the shaking she felt so deep within her core. She lifted her hand to the tightly coiled Bantu knots on her head and brushed imaginary loose strands back into place.

"What the hell am I doing?"

Less than ten minutes ago Dante was demanding answers from her. That was almost comical considering his actions were directly responsible for the crazy shit that had taken place in her life. If anyone was owed an explanation, it was her. Too bad the bossy Italian waiting in her living room didn't see it that way.

He wasn't going to drop this. Neither was she. The only difference—she was going to fight smart. Standing in the middle of her living room arguing with him wasn't going to win this for her.

In the middle of Dante's rant she'd held up a hand and told him, "I'm dirty and tired, and I'm not about to do this until I get clean. If you want answers, you're going to have to wait fifteen minutes." He hadn't liked it, but he'd stepped away and gave given her the space she needed to exit the room.

She'd believed the few minutes locked away in her bathroom would give her time to get her shit together. Too bad the joke was on her, because standing her alone in this room knowing Dante was waiting for her to explain herself was wreaking havoc on her nerves.

She gave herself a mental reprimand for standing there preening, for stalling. It was Dante, the man who'd nearly cost her everything, including her life. Why the hell should she care what he thought of her after all these years?

She pushed a long sigh out of her lungs and into the air. Who was she fooling? This wasn't about making sure she looked good in front of company. Well, not entirely, anyway. Yeah, she didn't want to look like a poor relation in front of Dante—especially since the last six years had done nothing but enhanced the fine that man wore naturally. But her primping in the mirror had more to do with avoidance than anything else.

"Sanai, you either come out here, or I'm coming in there, but either way, we're having this conversation now."

The strong rumble of his voice seemed to vibrate through the wood of the door and into her body. She tensed her muscles, trying to ward against the tremble that sound was igniting.

I am not afraid of him. I did what I had to. I am not afraid of him.

"Sanai!"

Wait, is he inside my room?

She grabbed the knee-length bathrobe hanging on the wall, pulled it on, and tied the sash quickly around her waist. Her suspicions were confirmed when she pulled the door open and saw him sitting comfortably on her bed.

The nerves she'd been battling inside the bathroom gave way to fiery anger, boiling quickly.

"'Fuck are you doing in here? I left you in the living room," she barked.

"Forgive me if I didn't trust you not to disappear through the bathroom window," he countered quietly.

She walked until she stood directly in front of him, chest heaving, head pounding with the sound of her heart banging against her ribs. "Who the fuck do you think you are?"

He stood up at the close of her question, his frame reaching just shy of six feet, solid, with thick muscles straining his shirt, forcing her to take a step back as she looked up at him.

"I'm the fucking man that loved you more than my own life!" he bellowed as he stepped forward, forcing her to backpedal with each step he took. "The man who thought he would die when I found a dead woman burned beyond recognition holding the locket I gave you, the locket you wore every day. I'm the fool that stood over a hole in the ground and cried like a baby at his mother's tit while a casket holding what I thought were your remains was lowered into it," he screamed.

Her back crashed against the hard wall, but she couldn't stop to worry about the zing of pain spreading against her shoulders and the back of her skull. Unsure of what he'd do, she needed to keep her eyes on him.

The Dante she'd known had never been a violent man—intense with a temper to be wary of, yes, but he'd never been violent.

It's been six years; can you still count on that?

When she was flat against the wall, he cornered her, both arms caging her as his palms rested on either side of her head. He leaned down closer to her, forcing his eyes to meet hers. "I'm the man who came back to that lonely grave every day for six fucking months, lying curled up on it because it was the only place I could be physically close to you."

The image of Dante lying in a dark cemetery aching for her tore something in Sanai. He might have been indirectly involved with why she'd left Florida the way she didhad, but no human being deserved that kind of mental and emotional torture. That was exactly what it was; the rage filling his fixed onyx stare was telling enough. There was so much anger there, anger that only came when you'd lost something irreplaceable.

His pupils were blown, his breathing ragged, large swells of air pushing in and out of his lungs. He wasn't speaking. She didn't even think he was capable of speaking any longer, rage vibrating off his trembling frame.

She took a shaky hand and touched the small patch of olive skin on his wrist exposed by his rolled-up sleeves.

"Dante, I..." She swallowed, attempting to think of what to say next. She'd had cause to be angry all these years, much of it focused on him. But she'd never entertained the idea that he'd suffered the way his outburst suggested.

She couldn't find the words, so she stroked that area of skin with slow, soft movements. She continued her circular strokes until his breathing calmed, until he began to blink away some of the rage clouding his soulful eyes. Until she believed he was seeing her and not his anger at her.

"Dear God... You're alive," he whispered. His eyes watered, and tears began to make a slow trek down the sharp angles of his face, joining into a huge drop at the bottom of his squared chin. "I prayed so many times just to be able to touch you again, feel your touch...hear your voice."

Tentative fingers danced over the edges of her jaw, across her cheeks and forehead, down the wide bridge of her nose. It was such a familiar pattern. Something she should've forgotten by now, something that should be deemed insignificant after all this time. It was how he would outline her face in the darkness of her bedroom after they'd made love, or when he was waking her up in the morning to make love to her again.

This path was always the same. No matter how many times he'd done it, it was always the same. And then his fingers landed on their final destination—her lips. He traced each of them with a slow, sacred pace, until her entire body was dancing with anticipation.

When her lips opened for him, as they had so many times before in the past, he pushed his thumb inside. His eyes locked with hers, and instinct took over. At least that was what she told herself as she closed her eyes and lips and sucked on the lone digit, tongue swirling around it, laving at it until she heard the tiny but familiar pull of breath he took into his lungs.

As soon as tongue touched skin, she felt the lips of her pussy swell with sensitivity, her desire beginning to pulse, her muscles pulling in an open-and-close motion. How could she be so fucking thirsty for someone she'd claimed to hate all this time?

He pulled his thumb from her mouth and placed it at the junction of her clavicles, allowing it to slide down the darkened line that traveled between her breasts and down her abdomen. He kept sliding that thumb down until it separated the loosely tied belt of her robe and allowed the two satin halves to fall away to her sides. He kept that thumb moving until it dipped inside her belly button, forcing her to draw in a breath to still herself.

She forced her eyes open, hoping to find some glimpse of the sanity she knew she was losing in his eyes, but the only thing that stared back was fire—fire she'd experienced, and God help her, fire she wanted to experience again.

His thumb continued its journey until it split her slick folds. It traveled down until it touched the pooling stream at her opening and traveled just a short way up again as it searched for treasure. The moment it made contact with her clit, her entire body shuddered. He must've taken that as permission, and if she were truly being honest, that was exactly what it was.

He grabbed her to him, hoisting her legs around his waist before taking her down to the floor. He climbed atop her, his thumb, now replaced by the middle and ring fingers of his left hand, circling around her clit. Her traitorous body sought his touch as she curled up against those fucking fingers, begging him to touch her, satisfy her.

Should you really be doing this, allowing this to happen?

There it was, the rational side of her brain. She'd figured it would show up sooner or later. It was just about to make her close her legs and push Dante off her when rough lips pressed against hers, bruising the skin there, forcing her to respond to that divine pressure. She made the mistake of trying to pull air into her lungs; the small opening of her lips was enough space for him to dip into her mouth with his tongue. Once he found entry, any notion she'd had of putting the brakes on this impromptu romp ended. She fell into the forceful motion his tongue was stroking out against hers.

She heard the fumbling of fabric, and something metallic. The next thing she knew, she felt him, really felt him, his hard, curved cock pressing against her entrance. A streak of panic sliced through the fog of desire until Sanai felt the latex barrier between them. At least he'd had sense to protect them both, something she'd make sure to reprimand herself about later, but right now—right now she was going to enjoy every hard and fast second of this.

And it would be hard...and fast. Dante had that look of determination carved into his features, the one that'd always told her when he was too hungry to make love to her nicely. This was about to be brutal, and she was so grateful it would be that way.

Six years since she'd walked away, only moments after he'd found her, and they were back to this again, back to this insane connection she'd thought would one day rob her of her ability to breathe. And now, all these years later she was still thinking the exact same thing.

This motherfucker is going to ruin me...again.

Coming Up Next In Lunchtime Chronicles

I t was supposed to be one night only...

They say it's easier to confide in strangers. And that's all Dr. Zina Washington was doing with the tall, dark and handsome bartender of the hotel where she's staying. Pouring her heart out, telling him about her a-hole ex, and how much she dreads seeing him the following day. She didn't expect her hot, attentive stranger would invite her to the hotel's penthouse suite and give her the best night of her life. Didn't expect they'd talk, laugh and go at it all night. But in the bright light of day, reason returns and Zina sneaks out.

Now her magical night is over, and she has to face her horrible ex and his new piece. Alone. Or does she?...

Tag along for a swoony and steamy instalove, instalust, curvy girl, BWWM, secret billionaire romance novella. No cheating, no cliffhanger, HEA guaranteed!